BOOTS
Optional

BECAUSE NAUGHTY CAN BE OH SO NICE®

NE LTD

By Nicole Edwards

The Alluring Indulgence Series
Kaleb
Zane
Travis
Holidays with the Walker Brothers
Ethan
Braydon
Sawyer
Brendon

The Austin Arrows Series
Rush
Kaufman

The Bad Boys of Sports Series
Bad Reputation
Bad Business

The Caine Cousins Series
Hard to Hold
Hard to Handle

The Club Destiny Series
Conviction
Temptation
Addicted
Seduction
Infatuation
Captivated
Devotion
Perception
Entrusted
Adored
Distraction

The Coyote Ridge Series
Curtis
Jared

The Dead Heat Ranch Series
Boots Optional
Betting on Grace
Overnight Love

By Nicole Edwards (cont.)

The Devil's Bend Series

Chasing Dreams
Vanishing Dreams

The Devil's Playground Series

Without Regret
Without Restraint

The Office Intrigue Series

Office Intrigue
Intrigued Out of the Office
Their Rebellious Submissive

The Pier 70 Series

Reckless
Fearless
Speechless
Harmless

The Sniper 1 Security Series

Wait for Morning
Never Say Never
Tomorrow's Too Late

The Southern Boy Mafia Series

Beautifully Brutal
Beautifully Loyal

Standalone Novels

A Million Tiny Pieces
Inked on Paper

Writing as Timberlyn Scott

Unhinged
Unraveling
Chaos

Naughty Holiday Editions

2015
201

BOOTS Optional

DEAD HEAT RANCH

Book 0.5

NICOLE EDWARDS

Nicole Edwards Limited
PO Box 806
Hutto, Texas 78634
www.NicoleEdwardsLimited.com

Cover Image: © Poulsons Photography | 123rf

Cover Design: © Nicole Edwards Limited
Editing: Blue Otter Editing | www.BlueOtterEditing.com

ISBN (ebook): 978-1-939786-25-8
ISBN (print): 978-1-939786-26-5

Romance

Mature Audiences

NOTE FROM AUTHOR:

This novella was previously published in the anthology, *Some Like It Hot*.

Please note, the story did not change, however, there is a short bonus scene at the end that involves Gracie's sister, Mercy. Hope you enjoy!

~Nic!

PROLOGUE

"WHAT THE HELL?" GRANT SLURRED as he stuck his head in the refrigerator, his plan for finding another beer not looking good. Either they'd already sucked them all down, or he was drunker than he thought. He doubted it was the latter, but the cool refrigerated air sweeping across his overheated skin told him he was feeling *something*.

Although "drunk" was a fantastic excuse, it wasn't likely the culprit.

"What's the problem?" Lane asked, poking his head damn near in the refrigerator beside Grant's, his powerful shoulder pressing up against his arm.

Grant jumped back, stumbled a couple of steps before he righted himself by grabbing the edge of the Formica countertop. He stared back at his friend, noticing the way Lane moved ever so slowly as he turned around to face Grant.

Yeah, that hadn't been at all subtle.

"Well, damn, Grant. I showered before I came over." Lane ducked his head near his armpit and sniffed. "Nope, I smell like an ocean breeze. Did you know that's what a fucking ocean breeze smells like?"

Grant fought the urge to smile. Lane did that to him. The man was always attempting to make him laugh but at the moment, he couldn't find much humor in the incredibly awkward situation he found himself in. "What're you talkin' about?" Grant asked, the room spinning just a little, but it had nothing to do with the alcohol swimming in his system.

Although he did need another beer. That or he needed for Lane to go home. Either option would work for him.

Shit.

Lane closed the refrigerator door just a little too hard, a couple of glass bottles clanking together as the door shut tight. Grant kept his eyes on the taller man, wishing like hell he hadn't opened the front door to let his friend in a couple of hours ago. Then again, everything had been fine as they sat in their respective recliners watching television up until about three minutes ago, but *no*, Grant had to go and need another beer.

Well, truthfully, everything *hadn't* been fine but at least Lane hadn't realized that. Grant was tense, but he seemed to always be that way around Lane. A reaction that had become increasingly more frustrating in recent months. Mostly due to the attraction he felt for the handsome wrangler who'd become one of his closest friends over the past couple of years.

"You got a problem with me, Kingsley?" Lane asked, his eyes dancing with amusement, his deep voice reverberating through Grant's entire body as the man moved closer. Incredibly close.

"Just need a beer," Grant said, his mouth suddenly dry.

"There's another six pack on the table." Lane motioned his head toward the kitchen table, his eyes never leaving Grant's face.

Grant made the mistake of looking over and sure enough, there was a six-pack of long neck bottles right there.

How the hell had he missed that?

When he looked back at Lane, the man was even closer. Close enough that yes, Grant was well aware that he had showered – and shaved – before he stopped by. He smelled good. Too good.

"You're actin' weird," Lane told him bluntly, tilting his head slightly as he studied Grant's face.

"Weird?" Grant asked stupidly, swallowing hard.

He wasn't acting weird. He was trying to drink himself into a stupor since that seemed to be the only way he could make it through any length of time around Lane without wanting to jump the man.

Snapping back to the present, Grant put his hands on Lane's chest, ready to shove his friend back because he was too damn close. Before he could do as much, Lane covered Grant's hands with his own, holding them to his chest and preventing Grant from putting any space between them.

Lane's heartbeat thudded rhythmically beneath Grant's palms.

Double shit.

"What are you doing?" Grant asked, though the words came out breathless and rough as he stared into Lane's dark, dark brown eyes.

"What do you think I'm doing?"

"Hell if I know," Grant lied. He knew exactly what Lane was doing and he'd be damned if he knew how to stop him, but that was only because he didn't *want* to stop him. Grant had dreamed about this moment, but he'd never thought it would actually happen.

Not with Lane. Not like this anyway.

Lane's chest was hard beneath his palms, his hands hot against the backs of his, and Grant found it rather difficult to breathe.

He hadn't had that much beer, damn it.

"Man, quit fucking with me," Grant bellowed, once again trying to push Lane away, pretending that he had no idea what was about to happen in three... two... one...

Oh, goddamn!

The instant Lane's mouth touched his, Grant lost all ability to shove him away; instead, he was reaching up, grasping Lane's hair in his fist and pulling him against him as the kiss exploded. Tongues, teeth, hands...

"Holy fuck," Lane mumbled long seconds later when he pulled back, looking directly into Grant's eyes before his mouth slammed into his once more.

Grant's entire body went hot, his cock hardening. And when Lane pushed up against him, successfully pinning Grant between the counter and his massive body, he was at a loss. The only thing he could do was kiss this man.

Kiss him and pray like hell that what they were doing wasn't the stupidest thing either of them had ever done.

□●□●□●□

TO PUT IT SIMPLY, LANE was shocked.

For one, he'd dreamed of this moment for months, never actually believing they would ever get to this point although they'd been doing some strange dance for about that long. Despite Grant's attempt to hide his desire, Lane had felt the heat of Grant's stare more than once.

And now, Grant had his hands in Lane's hair, pulling him closer while their tongues played hockey, dueling for control. Lane couldn't get enough of him. Grant tasted like beer and sex and – *holy fuck* – he wanted more.

With ease, Lane managed to spin them so that he was the one against the counter and Grant was in front of him. Holding him near while Grant continued to pull on his hair, Lane snaked his hand between their bodies and made quick work of releasing the button on Grant's jeans. Within seconds, he had the zipper down and Grant's jeans around his thighs. Oh, no, he wasn't going to let this moment go. Not if he had any say in the matter.

When Grant groaned, Lane wrapped his fingers around his thick cock, firmly gripping him. Just enough to let him know who was in control. Not that Lane had much control left. Not after tonight.

For nearly two hours, they'd sat in the living room laughing at the television while Grant had tried his best to ignore Lane at every turn. Lane knew how it worked, he knew what to expect from Grant, because the man wasn't going to outwardly pursue him, even if Lane begged. Yet here they were and his head was about to explode because he was touching Grant, kissing him.

Fuck. It was better than he anticipated.

"Holy shit," Grant moaned as he pulled back, his attention immediately turning to where Lane was stroking him slowly.

"Does it feel good?"

"Yeah," Grant breathed roughly. "Too good."

"And to think you've been avoiding this. Avoiding *me*."

Lane didn't need Grant to admit it, he already knew the truth. But he'd promised himself that if they ever got to this point, he wouldn't let the moment pass him by.

Something caught his eye and Lane looked up to see...

Christ. There in the doorway – behind Grant – was Gracie Lambert. She was staring at them, clearly mesmerized to the point she didn't realize Lane knew she was there.

What he wouldn't give for her to take a chance and erase the twenty or so feet that stood between her and pleasure the likes of which none of them had ever known. But he knew Gracie. She wasn't going to act on any impulse, no matter how tempting the urge might be. She had been blowing them off since day one, and Lane figured that if she had her way, she'd continue to do so until hell froze over.

"Lane," Grant moaned, his head falling back as Lane continued to stroke him.

"I want to taste you," Lane admitted, his eyes still locked on Gracie, but she wasn't looking up at him. She was completely unaware that he was watching her, which made it that much hotter.

Grant didn't tell him no. He didn't try to pull away and fuck it all, Lane just wanted to take him in his mouth and blow his mind. Something to ease the pressure in hopes that Grant would see that there was something between them even if he were scared to admit it.

Lane forced Grant back a couple of steps, enough to give him room to go to his knees on the worn linoleum floor. Looking up at Grant, Lane continued to stroke him while the cowboy watched, his ocean blue eyes glazed with desire.

With ease, he darted his tongue out and lapped at the bead of pre-cum slicking the head of Grant's engorged cock. Another growl from Grant, and Lane sucked him fully into his mouth, their eyes still locked together.

Although he wasn't looking directly at her, Lane could still feel Gracie watching them. It wasn't that he needed any damned encouragement because shit, Grant was more than enough to make Lane hot, but he would admit that knowing the woman was standing there, probably heating up nicely from the free show going on before her, didn't hurt.

Grant's strong hand slid into Lane's hair, holding him firmly as Lane continued to suck him deep and then retreat. Over and over, he continued to lave Grant's dick while he fondled Grant's balls with one hand.

"God, Lane. Fuck. I've wanted you to do this for a long damn time."

Lane didn't comment. He just sucked harder, deeper, faster.

"Fuck yes," Grant groaned, his hand clutching Lane's hair painfully tight, sending shards of electricity through his scalp. "God, don't stop. Don't ever fucking stop."

Grant didn't have to worry there. Lane had wanted to get his hands on Grant for a long damn time. He also wanted to get his hands on the sweet cowgirl still watching them from the shadows of the front porch. He'd openly admitted to the latter, but never had he out and out admitted the intensity of his desire for Grant.

Not until tonight.

"God damn," Grant howled. "You're gonna make me come. Fuck. You're gonna…"

That's exactly what Lane was going for. At least for tonight. Tonight was about Grant.

And the sexy cowgirl who might not yet realize just what she'd gotten herself into.

CHAPTER ONE

"I DON'T GIVE A DAMN what time he said he'd be here. I fuc–" Grace Lambert slammed her mouth closed, shutting down her own tirade before it was too late. As it was, she had...

"Abigail Grace Lambert! Watch your damn mouth!"

Yep, she'd gone and done it now. Pissing off her pop first thing in the morning probably wasn't the best way to start the day. In fact, she usually preferred a little caffeine before he chewed her a new one.

Probably to avoid her father's wrath, Casey – one of the wranglers who helped out in the kitchen each morning – hauled ass out the back door, the screen slamming shut behind him. Lucky bastard. Grace added *"Pay Casey back for bailing"* to her mental list of things to do today as she turned back to her father who'd puffed up like a bullfrog, getting ready to lay into her a little more.

"I did, Daddy!" she exclaimed before he could continue. Lowering her voice about ten decibels, she followed up with, "Sorry."

"What the hell's goin' on in here?"

The back door swung open and following that dark, rich Texas twang was none other than the bane of her existence, Grant Kingsley, Dead Heat Ranch's pain in the ass head foreman. He looked at Grace then back out the door probably at Casey running full out toward the bunkhouse to find the cook who apparently thought he was on vacation.

"Watch your mouth, Kingsley," Grace muttered beneath her breath as she poured her coffee, purposely not making eye contact. It was bad enough that the mere sight of him made her blush. Especially after... She had things to do, and the first thing on her agenda was to get away from Grant as soon as possible because she damn sure didn't have time to think about what she saw last Friday night.

"Yes, ma'am," Grant said in that silky drawl, his mouth much too close to her ear as he passed by her, using his quest for coffee as his excuse to touch her.

Grace did her damnedest to hide her unwelcome reaction to the cowboy who'd been working for her family's ranch for more years than she had been. "Where's Lane?" she asked, pretending she hadn't noticed how close he was.

"Haven't seen him yet this mornin'," Grant answered easily as he reached for a coffee cup in the cabinet above Grace's head. "You lookin' for him? I can see if I can locate him for you."

Holding her own cup with both hands, because yes, they were trembling slightly, she eased out from between the tall cowboy and the unyielding counter to join her father at the kitchen table. "Nope. Just hadn't seen him yet." *And wanted to make sure I didn't run into him too*, she thought to herself.

"Where's Faith?" Jerry Lambert asked, her father's question not directed at anyone in particular. Or so it seemed.

Grace sipped her coffee, once again pretending there wasn't another hot cowboy walking through the back door of the ranch's main house right about...

Now.

"Mornin'," Lane Miller greeted as the back door slammed behind him.

His ears must've been burning.

Doing what she did best, Grace ignored him too as she answered her father. "Don't know. She said she was stoppin' by first thing, but you know, it's only six-thirty. Some people like the sun to be up before they climb outta bed on Monday mornin'."

Grace hadn't seen her youngest sister since yesterday morning. In fact, she hadn't seen any of her sisters because she'd managed to spend her one day off during the week hiding out from everyone, including her family, but most importantly the two cowboys now hogging the coffee pot. Sunday was the only day she didn't work, and in order to stick to that promise she'd made to herself about taking time to relax, she refused to head to the main house for fear someone would put her to work.

Or that she'd run into these two.

It always happened that way.

"How's it goin', Lane?" Jerry greeted one of Dead Heat's few permanent wranglers, a man Grace tried to stay away from as much, if not more so, than Grant.

"Good, sir. Got a group coming in this mornin'. Plannin' a day ride."

Lane Miller had been working at Dead Heat Ranch for at least three years. For the most part, he handled the horses that they used for the trail rides. He also led those rides with the guests who frequented the place.

Did she mention that Dead Heat Ranch was a working dude ranch?

Grace's father didn't respond, just nodded his head. They were all used to it. The man ran one of Texas' largest dude ranches, but he said very little. Unless, of course, one of the guests pulled him into a conversation, then you could pretty much guarantee the man wouldn't shut up.

When she had drained her coffee, Grace pushed back her chair and got to her feet. Perfect timing too since Lane and Grant looked like they were settling in to stay awhile as they relaxed casually against the counter.

Rinsing her cup, she placed it in the dishwasher, murmured a good-bye to her father and snuck out the door as fast as her feet would take her.

Grace hadn't made it far when she heard the screen door slam once more. With her head down, she made a beeline for the barn, hoping like hell someone was there. Because if not, that meant she was about to find herself alone with one, or possibly two, nearly irresistible cowboys.

It's the way her mornings usually went.

"Grace! Hold up!"

"No thanks!" she hollered back, not bothering to look behind her. "Not interested in what you're sellin', cowboy!"

The sexy chuckle that followed belonged to Grant. She would recognize it just about anywhere.

Shit.

Grace stepped into the shadows of the barn about the same time Grant caught up to her.

"What's the rush?" he asked and thankfully, he didn't try to touch her, although he was close enough that she could smell the sexy scent of his aftershave.

"Workin'. You might try it sometime. I think it's why we pay you, right?" Grace was purposely trying to piss him off. It was the only way she could usually put some distance between the two of them.

And she had a damn good reason to put as much space between her and…

"Hey," Lane called, stepping into the barn just a few feet behind Grant.

… him.

Crap.

Double trouble. That's what these two were.

"Go on, Gracie," Grant taunted. "Give Lane your '*you should be workin'*" speech. He's waitin'."

"Shut up."

Sometimes she felt like a cantankerous teenager when these two were around. Especially Grant. She'd known him for more years than she could remember. He was, at thirty-two, only a few years older than she was, but at the ripe old age of twenty-eight, Grace knew she should be long past the stage where she went on the defensive with these two annoying cowboys. After all, she had managed to fend them off for... Well, forever.

And okay, so they weren't so much annoying as they were relentless. But just like she had told Grant, she wasn't buying what they were selling. Mainly because she had no idea what they *were* selling. Or to who they were selling it. Based on what she'd seen just a few days ago, she wasn't sure she had the right anatomy to fulfill either one of them.

"She's back to that?" Lane asked in that laid-back, country drawl that didn't fool her at all.

Just as she did every morning, Grace moved toward Astro Boy's stall. It was the first item on her daily to-do list. Astro Boy was her five-year-old paint horse, and he was hers and hers alone which was why she came to check on him every morning and again every afternoon. That was if she didn't spend part of the day riding him around the ranch.

Although Dead Heat Ranch had a number of horses, most of them were geldings that they used for the trail rides with the guests. And due to the fact the guests were restricted to the more docile horses, no one was allowed to ride Astro Boy. And he knew it, too.

"Hey, boy," she greeted him with a grin as she pushed open the metal stall door that kept him safely inside. Just seeing him could turn her mood from bad to good in an instant. "Miss me?"

She received a heavy snort and a nudge in response. Grace placed her palm flat on his wide nose and smiled up at him.

"*I* did," Grant answered, although her question definitely hadn't been directed at him.

Grace ignored him; instead, making her way into Astro Boy's stall as she took his brush and went to work.

All hope of the two men going on about their business died when Lane came to stand beside Grant, both of them leaning casually against the inner wall of the stall. Glancing up, she noticed that Lane was, in fact, standing incredibly close to Grant. She quickly looked away, hoping they couldn't read her mind.

Because if they could, they would probably realize that their secret was out.

□●□●□●□

GRANT KINGSLEY COULDN'T TAKE HIS eyes off Gracie. Then again, that was a problem he'd had for quite a few years. And it wouldn't be a problem if the woman would just pay a little attention to him. He knew she wanted to. It was in her eyes when she looked at him. That damn sure wasn't indifference he saw in her blue-green gaze.

That was lust.

But for the better part of the last few years, Gracie Lambert had successfully dodged every single one of Grant's advances. She'd dodged Lane's too, but Grant figured she had no idea they'd knowingly been pursuing her simultaneously. Then again, how could she know? Although it certainly hadn't started out that way.

It started out innocently enough – if two competitive cowboys, a twelve pack of beer, a game of pool, and an obnoxious bet could be considered innocent. Regardless, that night, Grant and Lane had agreed that, since they were both vying for the pretty cowgirl's affections, they'd see who could win a date with her first.

That was two years ago.

Yeah. For two fucking years, they'd been trying *and* failing to get Gracie Lambert to admit to her attraction to them. Neither of them had made it even remotely close to getting a date with the beautiful woman though.

That hadn't stopped them from trying.

"Look, boys, I've got things to do today. So if you don't mind," Gracie said without looking up at them.

"I don't mind. Do you mind?" Lane asked with his usual laidback excitement. "Cuz I could stand here all day and enjoy the view. I don't mind watching. I happen to like it actually. Unless of course, you'd just like to say you'll go out with me. Then I'll back off. And I'll pick you up at seven."

Grant glanced over at Lane. He was rambling more than usual and that was saying something. Once he got started, the guy didn't usually let up. For some strange reason, Grant found that trait oddly appealing.

Gracie clearly didn't if the frown on her pretty face was anything to go by.

"Lay off," Gracie bit out, her eyes slamming into Lane's face before they crashed into Grant's a moment later.

Crap. They'd gone and pissed her off again.

Gracie wanted them to believe that everything they did pissed her off, but Grant had been around long enough to know that the woman wasn't mad. At least not at them. She was mad at herself because she liked them. Maybe not enough to fall into bed with either of them, but Gracie certainly didn't hide her attraction as well as she probably hoped she did. Which was the main reason Grant didn't back off, even when she insisted.

However, he wasn't opposed to making her believe she'd won.

"All right, we'll lay off," Grant told her. "I really just wanted to ask if you were making a trip into town today."

Gracie looked up at him, her golden eyebrows downturned. Ever the skeptic that woman.

"*What?* You said last week that you had to head into town. I happen to know that your truck hasn't moved since last Thursday, so I thought I'd ask. I just needed a couple of things."

"Fine. Yes, I'm going into town. Give me a list of what you need and I'll pick it up for you."

"Thanks, Gracie." Grant retrieved a folded piece of paper from his pocket and held it out for her to take while Lane pinned him with a glare. Nope, he hadn't told Lane about this.

True to form, she didn't bother reading what was on his list; instead, she stuffed it into the front pocket of her jeans. "I'll catch back up with you this afternoon. Come on," he said to Lane, tilting his head toward the door. "I'll help you get ready for today's ride."

"What was on your list?" Lane asked when they were back out in the sunlight.

"Nothin' important," Grant lied, unable to look at Lane directly for fear the other man would see just what Grant was thinking. Or worse, feeling.

After what happened Friday…

"You know she's never gonna come around, don't you?"

Grant wasn't about to answer that. He knew nothing of the sort. For as long as he could remember, Grant had been pining away for Gracie Lambert. And yes, he knew just how fucking pathetic that sounded. But there it was. The cold, hard truth.

Grant had first arrived at Dead Heat Ranch thirteen years ago. He'd been a dumbass nineteen-year-old when he stumbled across an ad in the paper looking for summer help on a dude ranch. He wasn't even sure what a dude ranch was at the time, but shit, he'd been young and dumb and was hoping for some quick cash in his pocket.

Little did he know, but the moment he met Jerry Lambert and his five darling daughters, he was about to embark upon something that would change his life forever. The last thirteen years had been a blur. Somewhere along the way, he'd learned the ropes better than ol' Jerry had obviously expected, and now he found himself as the head foreman of the second biggest dude ranch in the state of Texas. It was a dream job, one he'd never expected to fall into.

He spent his day doing what he loved. The only downside was the three to four hours a month – and that was the worst case – that he spent behind a desk. He preferred to be outside, in the brilliant Texas sun, sweating his ass off while working with the animals, teaching the new guys the ropes, checking in with the guests, following up on what needed following up on. That was his life. There was no nine-to-five for him. Hell, most of the time he wasn't sure when he was working versus when he wasn't, but he wouldn't have it any other way.

So, there he was, going along, day after day for nearly ten years when all of a sudden he looked up and there was little Gracie Lambert. But she wasn't little anymore. No, she was all grown up and more strikingly beautiful than he'd thought possible. When he first met her, she'd been fifteen and as much of a pain in the ass as her sisters. Don't get him wrong, they all worked their asses off. Especially Gracie. She'd been doing twice as many chores as most of the wranglers even at that young age, but she'd been a rebellious teenager. All of the Lambert girls were. Rebellious that is. Yet, he had no idea when that had changed. Sure, she was a smartass and quite defensive, but the woman was nothing like the teenage girl had been.

That was about the time her daddy opted to give every cowboy at the ranch a talkin' to. The one that started with… "Stay the fuck away from my daughters." And ended the exact same way.

It hadn't deterred Grant. Well, except for the fact that he now kept his interest on the down low. More so than before.

But it was pretty much irrelevant because, no matter how hard he tried to convince Gracie to give him a chance, the woman hardly looked at him. Then again, that was partly his fault. For the last... God, he didn't even know how long it had been. The only thing he knew was that about the same time as when he'd been laid for the first time, Grant had been rocked by a shocking realization that he hadn't expected and certainly hadn't understood.

Then again, he was still confused by it, but he'd learned to live with it. It was who he was.

Yeah, Grant's biggest secret was that he was bisexual. Not gay. Not straight.

No, his life wasn't that straightforward. It would certainly be easier if he swung one way or the other. Not both. But, after spending a few years denying it, then another few years assuming he was gay, Grant had learned he happened to like both men and women. Equally.

What did that mean? If fucking meant that Gracie Lambert made his dick hard. And so did Lane Miller. And wasn't that just a bunch of fucked up. Not that Grant had been attracted to Lane all that time because at first, they'd just been friends.

Grant didn't go around sharing his secret with just anyone. So, for the most part, no one knew he was just as interested in men as he was women. He'd learned that lesson early on. Share too much and people look at you sideways.

But Lane knew. Obviously. He knew and he didn't seem to care. One of Dead Heat's best wranglers wasn't shy about who he was either. And strangely enough, Lane didn't seem at all worried that Grant had ogled him a time or two. Or twenty.

Of course not. Lane Miller was the most confident cowboy Grant had ever met. At six-feet-three-inches, with thighs like redwood trees, an upper body that filled out a T-shirt to its max, and lips that...

Nope, Grant wasn't going to go there.

Fuck.

Nonetheless, Lane was quite confident in himself. Dark hair, even darker eyes, and always sporting a clean-shaven jaw, the man drew attention without even trying. And when he was drunk, the guy obviously didn't give a fuck who he was with.

Or at least that's the impression Grant got.

They hadn't been close for long. Maybe for the last six months or so. Before then it'd been a competition between them – who could get Gracie first. But during that time, Grant had obviously sparked something in Lane because last Friday night, after they had both spent far too much time with their good buddies Bud and Coors, Lane had kissed him.

Fucking kissed him and given him the best fucking blowjob of his entire fucking life.

"You all right?" Lane asked him now, pulling him – *thank God* – from that memory.

"Yeah, why?"

"I asked you a question, man."

Shit. "Sorry, what's up?"

"What are you doin' for dinner tonight?"

Grant came to a halt, glancing around to see who was near, praying like hell that no one had heard that question.

"Shit. Relax, man. It's fucking dinner. Either we eat it out of a fucking can or we stop by the kitchen and grab something with the guests. I wasn't asking you out on a date."

For whatever reason, that last part slammed against Grant's chest as though Lane had sucker punched him, nearly knocking the wind right out of him. A date? Had he really thought that?

"Fuck," Lane bit out, yanking his straw hat from his head and running his fingers through the unruly dark strands that were just a little too long. A little too sexy. "About last Friday…"

"Nuh-uh. Don't fucking go there," Grant bit out, turning to walk away. The next thing he knew, Lane was grabbing his arm hard enough to turn him around.

"Don't walk away, Kingsley," Lane growled, his voice low. "Don't fucking do that."

"I'm not gonna do this here," Grant whispered. He wasn't going to do this *anywhere*, but he didn't have to tell Lane that. It was one thing for people to know they were interested in the same woman, but it was something entirely different for people to think they were interested in… fuck. For them to be interested in each other.

Not happening.

Not here on the ranch. No fucking way.

Pulling away from Lane, he glared back at the man. "I've got shit to do. I'll catch you later."

LANE WATCHED GRANT WALK AWAY. Confusion wracked him at the reaction he had to the other man. So much so, he didn't hear Hope Lambert, Gracie's oldest sister, walk up.

"You ready? Or are you gonna stand here with your thumb up your ass all day?"

Forcing his expression to be blank, Lane turned and looked at Hope. The woman looked so much like her four sisters it was eerie. All five sisters sported long blonde hair, usually pulled back in a ponytail when they were working, those fascinating blue-green eyes, and they were all petite. They all were the spitting image of their mother, who had, unfortunately, passed away when the girls were still really young.

But their looks and their ambitious work ethic were about the only thing they had in common. As far as personalities, they were very different.

"Let me pull my thumb out and I'll be right there," Lane snarled back at Hope.

"You do that."

Lane didn't miss the fact that Hope was looking at him funny.

Taking a deep breath, Lane turned on his boot heels and followed Hope out to the stable. They'd tasked three of the temporary wranglers with getting the geldings ready for the ride today. Late last week, a rather large group from a local bank had scheduled some sort of team building event. They thought that horseback riding would be an appropriate way to get to know each other better apparently, and they were to arrive... Lane consulted his watch. Shit, they were going to be there in half an hour and he had no clue whether the horses were going to be ready or not.

Catching up to Hope, he tried to force Grant and Gracie out of his head. Easier said than done considering he'd been thinking about the two of them for the last few months. Okay, so that was a damn lie. Lane had been thinking about the two of them for the last two years. Or more. But, until Friday night, he'd also been under the impression that he was the only one who was interested in a little more than seeing who could get a date with Gracie first.

The bottom line: Lane needed to get laid. Pure and simple.

It'd been... Fuck, it had been almost three months since that last fucked up encounter with the bar bunny whose name he couldn't remember. Just like Friday, credit for that little clusterfuck could be given to a case of beer and no dinner. The perfect blend of *mess-your-mind-up-optimism*.

Yeah, Lane had sworn off that whole *get-drunk-to-pretend-otherwise* shit and he'd been doing a damn good job of it until last Friday.

Dumbass.

"Come on, Lane. Get your head in the game. We've got shit to do," Hope hollered.

Yeah, he definitely needed to get his head in the game. Because otherwise... He was going to find himself in way over his head.

CHAPTER TWO

LANE WAS STARVING. HE'D HAD the day from hell and at the moment, he just wanted something hot and then maybe a cold shower before he fell into bed. At this point, he wasn't even going to bother with trying to find Grant.

For the better part of the last six freaking hours, Lane had pretty much entertained a group of horny women all by himself. Oh, yeah, after about ten minutes with the women, Hope had bowed out gracefully, telling them that something had come up but that they'd be in Lane's very capable hands. At that point, his *very capable hands* had wanted to throttle her. Those women were worse than a horde of kindergartners with their constant questions. "Have you always been a cowboy, Lane?" "Do you ride horses every day?" "How many cowboys work here?" "Are they all real cowboys?" "Are you currently riding anything else, Lane?"

Yes. Yes. A lot. Yes. *What?*

Those were his answers. It had been a long day of single word responses and now he was all talked out.

But that had just been the introductory discussion. From that point on, the ladies had pummeled him with more outlandish questions. And by the end of the ride, he just wanted to sneak off by himself which was a first for him. Lane always enjoyed taking the guests out, spending time with them. Sharing dinner afterward. He'd even been known to take a few of the hotties on midnight rides – without the horse.

"Have you seen Grant?"

Lane spun around to see Gracie walking toward him at a fast clip. The anger that radiated from her was palpable, yet it didn't mar the perfection that was her face.

Goddamn the woman was pretty.

They all were. Grace, Hope, Trinity, Mercy and Faith. All five of the Lambert sisters had been blessed with beauty beyond reason. They took after their mother, thank God. Good ol' Jerry wasn't a bad looking man, but he'd make a damn ugly woman.

"No," Lane told her as he braced himself for impact. She looked like she was ready to throw down with him right there in the dirt. She didn't seem to care that he was at least twice her size.

"Well, you tell him…"

Gracie didn't finish her sentence, but he could tell she had a few choice words for Grant. Her hands were balled into fists at her sides and she was biting her bottom lip. And damn it all to hell, Lane's cock was paying attention.

"Tell him *what?*" Lane asked, curious as to what the problem was.

"Never mind," she bit out.

When she went to stomp away, Lane found himself doing something he'd rarely ever done before. At least not intentionally. He actually touched her and it wasn't just an innocent brush of his arm against hers either. As if in slo-mo, Lane reached out and placed his hand on her arm, her warm skin so much softer and smoother than he anticipated. When she turned to face him, he jerked his hand back as though he'd been burned.

Okay, so he had always been attracted to her, but then again, what man wouldn't be? She was gorgeous. Long blonde hair, perfect bow-shaped lips, a tight, compact little body, and those smiling eyes. Yes, even when she didn't want to, her eyes seemed to smile. No matter how angry the woman tried to be at him or Grant, she always seemed to be secretly thinking about something else. Something that amused her.

But right now, her eyes weren't smiling. They were wide as she stared back at him, glancing down briefly to look at the place where he'd touched her arm and then back up to him.

Did she feel it too? Whatever that weird electrical charge was? Surely not. That was only something they spouted about in those racy books Gracie's older sister Hope liked to read.

"What's goin' on?"

Oh, hell. Lane looked up to see Grant making his way over and he knew that the shit was about to hit the fan.

And this time he was going to be the one to sit back and watch the action.

□●□●□●□

"GRANT KINGSLEY, YOU ARE A first-class asshole!" Grace shouted. She hoped like hell her daddy wasn't around because he was going to be pissed at the language she used, but she couldn't help herself.

After what Grant did... The nerve!

"What's wrong?" Grant asked, looking sincerely perplexed about her outrage.

"How dare you write something like that on that paper?"

Grant's face contorted from worry to amusement right before her very eyes. "Did you like that?"

"My sister did! She found it quite amusing, thank you very much."

The blasted man had the decency to blush.

"Oh, shit."

"'Oh, shit' is right," Grace spat back at him. "Now Faith thinks we've got something going on and she won't leave me alone about it." Upon reading Grant's clearly vulgar list of things he needed from town, Faith had a field day giving Grace shit about it.

"What did it say?" Lane asked, a huge grin on his too handsome face.

"You don't want to know," Grace told him snidely as she turned her attention back to Grant. "How dare you do that?"

"You were supposed to be the one to read it, Gracie. Not your sister."

"Well, she was more than happy to read it *to* me. Let's see if I remember it correctly. One: condoms. Two boxes, please. And the please was underlined. Two: chocolate syrup. And you even gave me delivery instructions. What was it? I was supposed to deliver those items to your cabin. Naked," Grace huffed before she continued, "Was that all? Did I leave something out?"

"Wine."

"*What?*"

"You forgot the wine. That was the first thing on the list. The condoms were number two."

Grace stared at him incredulously. Did he really think this was funny?

"Come on, Gracie. It was supposed to be a joke," Grant told her as he once again looked to be trying to hide his smile.

"So not funny," she told him.

"Why didn't you read it before you gave it to her?" Grant asked.

"Because I didn't expect that!"

"If you had, would you have read it?" Lane asked.

Grace turned her attention to him. "No. I wouldn't have." Okay, so maybe she would have, but they didn't need to know that. In truth, she had forgotten all about the list until Faith told her she needed to run into town. It was then that she remembered Grant's morning request, so she'd handed off the letter not realizing it was going to come back and bite her in the ass.

She was so pissed. Mainly because Faith had gone on and on about the fact that Grant Kingsley wanted her in his bed. Grace had endured the atrocious *"Gracie and Grant, sittin' in a tree, K-I-S-S-I-N-G."* from her twenty-five year old little sister.

It had been one of the most embarrassing moments of her life. Luckily, it had been Faith who had volunteered to go into town and not her dad. Christ, she didn't even want to think about what that would've been like. Her father would've skinned Grant alive and strung him up on the front gate as a warning to the rest of the cowboys on the ranch.

Unable to look at either of them any longer, Grace turned and stormed off. She wasn't hungry anymore. Not that she'd come looking for food in the first place. She'd been in search of Grant. And now that she'd found him and given him a piece of her mind, she was done.

So done.

"Gracie, wait!" Grant called.

"Dude, let her go." Lane's voice sounded far away.

Good, maybe he'd keep Grant there with him.

At least one of them had some common sense.

□●□●□●□

GRANT KNEW HE SHOULD PROBABLY be ashamed based on Gracie's reaction to his note. Or more importantly, the fact that Faith, Gracie's little sister, had read it.

He wasn't. Ashamed.

Then again, he was tired of this damn chase. He knew that his list didn't come as a surprise to her. He'd first started by asking her out. Several times over the last two years. She always played it off as if he were joking.

He wasn't.

Not one bit.

Bet be damned.

"Hold up. Where are you going?" Lane asked, his hand landing on Grant's shoulder, effectively pulling him back.

Hell, Grant hadn't even realized he'd started walking.

"I've got to go talk to her."

"Not right now you don't."

"Yes, I do. I've got to calm her down."

"Man," Lane laughed, "I don't think that's possible. Not unless maybe we sandwich her between us and–"

Grant's eyes opened wide as Lane cut off his words midsentence.

"Oh, hell. Would you look at that? It's time for dinner," Lane said quickly and turned toward the main house.

It was Grant's turn to stop him. But he didn't touch him. He couldn't bring himself to do it. "What did you say?"

"Shit." Lane dropped his head, but he didn't turn back to face Grant.

They stood there in silence for a moment, the sun falling just beneath the hills on the west side of the ranch. Damn, it was getting late. Summer in Texas meant the days were long. And hot. Unfortunately, these days, his nights were just as long, but definitely not hot. Not unless you counted last Friday night but even that midnight heatwave hadn't lasted but a few minutes.

Lane turned slowly and Grant kept his eyes on him. He was met with an expression he didn't recognize on Lane's face. Regret, maybe?

With his voice lowered to a barely audible volume, Lane asked, "Do you not remember *anything* from last Friday? Anything we talked about? Anything we *did*?"

Fuck. Fuck. Fuck.

Grant didn't break the eye contact. He held his breath. He knew exactly what Lane was referring to and goddammit, yes, he remembered it. He remembered everything. He wasn't nearly as drunk as he'd pretended to be.

"That's what I thought," Lane ground out, his eyes narrowing. "I'll catch you later."

"Wait," Grant growled before Lane turned away. "Just fucking wait."

Lane didn't move. Neither did Grant. They just stood there staring at one another for the longest time. Grant had no idea what to say. He was confused. Consumed by a mix of fear and anticipation, longing and dread.

"Will y'all just kiss already and get it over with?"

Grant's head snapped in the direction of the woman walking toward them as though his neck were made of rubber. Lane's did, too.

"Oh, come on," Mercy teased. "We all see it. You might as well just get it over with. Ain't like this is Brokeback Mountain or some shit. We couldn't be more pro equality for all if we flew a rainbow flag next to the Texas flag at the gate." Mercy laughed.

"What the fuck are you talking about?" Grant asked, unable to keep the dangerous tone from his voice.

He should've expected such a cheap shot from Mercy. Of the five Lambert sisters, she was the troublemaker.

"Lighten up. I'm teasin'," she said sweetly as she moved up close to them. "I've seen the way you boys look at Gracie. If it weren't for that, I'd think you two have a thing for each other. Y'all comin' to dinner?" Mercy had apparently moved on and was turning toward the house.

"Yeah, we'll be there in a minute," Lane offered, rotating to stand on Grant's side so he could look directly at Mercy, too.

"See ya." With that, they both watched Mercy walk away.

"I gotta go talk to Gracie," Grant said, not bothering to look at Lane. He wasn't in a position to explain anything right now and this wasn't the time or place to get into a conversation about what had happened last Friday night.

"I'm coming with you."

"No. You're not," Grant argued. "I've got to apologize."

Lane leveled his gaze on Grant, making him feel every ounce of the pure alpha he knew Lane to be. "I am."

Grant couldn't argue further. Not when Lane looked at him like that. Not when this man made him want things that he'd been denying himself for far too long as it was.

CHAPTER THREE

GRACE SLAMMED HER FRONT DOOR hard enough to rattle the windows. Standing just inside the living room of her small, one bedroom cabin, she took a deep breath.

Damn that man!

Truthfully, she wasn't really sure why she was so pissed. Except it gave her a damn good reason to put distance between the cowboy who had plagued her dreams for the last few months. She hadn't wanted Grant to show up and torment her in her sleep; that much she knew for sure. But he had anyway. Sort of like the living, breathing man, the dream version of Grant Kingsley was just as persistent. And just like the real man, he made her ache.

That didn't explain – AT ALL – why Lane Miller had shown up in her dreams as well starting several months ago. And there was that one dream where she actually kissed them both. Right there while they'd been sitting in her living room.

Like she would ever let them in her house.

Bang. Bang. Bang.

Grace nearly jumped out of her skin as the pounding on her front door rattled her teeth.

"Open the door, Gracie."

"No," she bit out obstinately, turning to face the door as though she could see Grant through the wood.

"It's not a request, darlin'."

That had her grabbing the doorknob and flinging the door open ready to blast him with what she thought about being told what to do.

"That's what I thought."

Grant was holding the screen door open and he stepped right inside as if he owned the place. And before she could shut the door on him, Lane was right behind him, one big hand holding the door open so that neither of them would receive a splinter in their face.

"What the fuck?" Taking two steps back, she stared at the two men looming over her.

The door closed behind Lane.

"Such a mouth," Lane said teasingly.

"Fuck off."

Lane took a step toward her, closing the distance between them, and Grace had to strain her neck to look up at him. He was at least a foot taller than she was and standing so close, he blocked her view of anything else.

"Such dirty words for such a pretty girl," Lane whispered, his voice dangerously close to seductive.

Grace didn't say anything. She couldn't. Her breath was lodged in her chest the moment Lane's warm fingers came up and caressed her cheek.

"There it is again," he mumbled absently.

"What?"

Lane took a step back while shaking his head, his hand dropping to his side as he stared at her like she'd sprouted a horn from her head.

"Gracie," Grant said. She looked his way in time to see his eyes bouncing between the two of them curiously. "We... No, *I* came over to apologize."

"Not necessary," she said breathlessly. Damn it.

"It is."

"No. It's not. Now if you'll just go. I'd like to..." *Go to bed.*

She definitely wasn't going to say that with these two standing there. Lord knew where they'd take that innocent comment. And she apparently didn't have the wherewithal to deal with either of them at the moment because she was trying to filter her thoughts.

"Gracie," Grant said her name again and she turned the full brunt of her frustration on him.

"*Grant.* I don't want to hear it. I don't want to play your stupid games, all right. I don't need you," she tilted her head toward Lane, "or *him* fucking with me right now. I get it. I haven't had a date in... God. I don't know how long it's been, but I don't need your pity. I don't need..."

Grace stopped talking as Grant stalked toward her. He was big and powerful and... So damn hot.

"Does this feel like pity?" Grant asked as he pressed up against her. He wasn't trying to intimidate her, but he was obviously attempting to make his presence known.

Message received. Loud. And. Clear.

"This damn sure ain't about pity, Gracie. And I *am* going to apologize. I didn't know your sister would read that list. It was meant for your eyes only. As a joke. And yeah, so maybe you'd get that I'm serious."

"Serious? Telling me to bring condoms and chocolate syrup to your house *and* deliver them naked, mind you... That's what you consider serious?"

"No, this is."

Grant kissed her.

And holy crap, her body ignited right there in the middle of her living room, the smoke could probably be seen for miles. He kissed her and kissed her and... Oh, God. She was kissing him back.

By the time Grant pulled back, Grace had shamelessly slid her hands into his hair, knocking his hat askew.

"Tell me you didn't feel that," Grant stated roughly, when he pulled away, his blue eyes boring right into her.

Grace was tempted to pretend she had no idea what he was talking about, but yeah… She came up blank.

□●□●□●□

"*I* FELT IT," LANE OFFERED when the only thing he could hear was the roar in his own ears from watching the two of them kiss. The rumble of his blood through his veins was even louder than their combined labored breaths.

Neither of them paid him any attention.

Fuck.

He knew he should turn around. He should just open the door, walk out into the warm June night, and forget all of the urges he had right at that moment.

Like the urge to kiss Gracie.

Or the urge to kiss Grant.

Oh, fuck.

Gracie must've found her wits because she pushed Grant away as she managed to put at least a foot between herself and either of them. "Why'd you do that?" The exasperation in her tone was enough to push Grant back a step. Lane held his ground. At least for now she wasn't aiming her ire at him.

"I've wanted to do that for a long damn time, Gracie." Grant's tone was serious. Lane could tell the man was not playing games.

Then again, he knew just what that felt like, because last Friday night, Grant had looked at him the exact same way right before he'd damn near blown Lane's mind with a kiss to rival all kisses. It didn't matter that Lane had been the one to instigate that explosive lip lock.

And yep, Lane would be the first to admit, he'd had more than his fair share of kisses. From men and women alike. He was bisexual, he didn't discriminate, and no, thanks to more than enough shit in his life, he'd spent years not being all that particular about who he spent his time with.

Until he started working at Dead Heat Ranch.

Since then he'd changed. A lot.

And yes, a lot of it had to do with these two people standing right there in front of him.

The two of them combined made him want to be a better man. Wow, now *that* sounded like a stupid cliché. But hell, if it weren't for them, he'd probably be working at a fast food joint right about now because he'd have burned more bridges than their small county even had.

"Have you always wanted to kiss *him* too?" Gracie asked, and Grant's eyes opened wide.

Lane's nearly bugged out of his head too, so yeah, his friend managed to maintain his composure significantly better than he was. Sure, Lane had known Gracie had watched them, but to hear her call them on it wasn't quite what he expected.

"Yes. Does that bother you?"

Holy fuck.

Lane stared at Grant, his mouth hanging open. He looked like an idiot, he was sure, but shit. What the hell else was he supposed to do? You damn sure weren't supposed to tell a chick you wanted to get with that you've wanted to kiss a guy.

They generally didn't take it well.

"So fucking with me is just for sport?"

See. Perfect example.

"No one's fucking with you, Gracie. Goddammit!" Grant yanked his Stetson off his head and slammed it against his jean-clad leg, turning away from Gracie.

"Sorry if I just don't understand, Grant. Why don't you explain it to me, huh? Tell me how it is that you want to kiss *both* of us? Are you that hard up? Or can you just not make up your mind?"

Well, hell.

Lane was damn glad he wasn't in Grant's boots right about now.

□●□●□●□

IF THERE WAS A MANUAL on how to seduce a woman, Grant needed it. Stat.

He was going down fast and he knew it.

Then again, if he'd known that Gracie had been snooping where she didn't belong on Friday, he might've gone about this differently.

Oh, shit. That meant she'd also seen… "Wait. Why were you at my cabin?"

Gracie didn't speak and he knew she was trying to come up with an excuse.

"Why, Gracie? Why'd you come to my cabin?" It was an important question because, in all of the years he'd been hot for this woman, she had stayed as far away from him as possible. So why wasn't she copping to it now?

"It doesn't matter. What matters is that the two of you were pretty hot and heavy which was probably why you didn't answer the door when I knocked."

"Bullshit," Grant argued. "The door was fucking open. You didn't need to knock."

He was stalling now, too. He knew it.

And no, he wasn't confused, but he knew it didn't matter what he told her, she was going to use it against him.

Yes. He had kissed Lane. Fuck yes; he liked the shit out of it, too. And hell, when Lane had sucked his dick Grant had been floating on a fucking cloud. Even hours after that, after Lane had gone back to his own cabin.

Closing his eyes as he smashed his hat back onto his head, Grant realized he should've been telling her all of these things.

Turning slowly, he glanced at Lane first, then Gracie.

"It's complicated."

"I'll say," Lane spouted. Always a damn comedian.

"Is that what you want too?" Gracie asked, this time her question directed at Lane.

"What? Both of you? Shit yeah."

Okay, so it clearly wasn't all that complicated for Lane.

Grant pinned him with a glare. He wasn't helping.

"Both of us?" Gracie's voice had lowered to tolerable levels as she stared up at Lane, her pretty pink mouth open. "Are you... Serious?"

"Hell yeah," Lane said.

Sometimes Grant wished he had the confidence Lane had. For as long as he'd known him, the man spoke his mind. Not that that was always a good thing. But at least he didn't keep it all bottled up the way Grant did.

Grant looked up to see Gracie staring back at him. An *"Is this guy serious?"* expression on her heart shaped face. Grant shrugged. And okay, that didn't help at all.

"Please leave," Gracie finally said. "I... I don't have time for this shit."

It was Lane's turn to address the situation apparently because he stalked Gracie the same way Grant had when he'd first walked in. The big man didn't stop until Gracie's back came in contact with the wall that separated her living room from her bedroom.

Do not think about her bedroom, asshole.

Yup. He was now thinking about her bedroom.

Gracie lying prone on the bed, gloriously naked, Lane between her thighs...

Oh, fucking shit.

Grant was pretty sure he was having a heart attack.

"Sweet thing," Lane told Gracie as he pulled his hat off his head.

That's all he said. Two words. And Gracie was looking up at him as though she were about to consume him whole.

And then Lane kissed her.

The emotion that rendered Grant speechless wasn't jealousy, but that's about all he knew. As he watched, Lane plundered her mouth, his big hand gripping her thigh and pulling her leg up almost to his hip as he ground against her. And Gracie was fully on board, her arms circled around his neck as she attempted to climb his body.

"Holy fuck," Lane whispered, his eyes still on Gracie as he pulled back.

"That's the same thing you said when you kissed him," Gracie spouted, pushing Lane away.

Damn the woman was giving some serious mixed signals here. She'd just kissed them both like she wanted to have them for dessert, yet she was still pushing them away. Then again, they were sort of tag teaming her. Which really wasn't fair.

Grant had spent plenty of time thinking about this scenario. It usually came about when he was ready to throw in the towel because it was clear, neither of them were going to get a date with this woman.

Or so he'd thought before tonight.

But now, there were so many questions running through his mind. But not one of them was how would it work or how would they get to this point? Those questions no longer needed answers because somehow, they were already here and in the span of five minutes, they had both kissed Gracie.

And that wasn't the only surprise. Grant hadn't figured he would just out and out tell her that he wanted to kiss her as much as he wanted to kiss Lane, but he'd been blinded by what she made him feel. It was potent.

"You were watchin' us, Gracie," Lane stated. Grant realized it wasn't a question at about the same time Lane continued. "Did you like what you saw? The way I pressed up against Grant, my cock rubbing against his through our jeans. Or were you more fixated on the way I inhaled him when I finally got my mouth on him? Or how about when I sucked his dick? Huh? Which was it?"

"Don't be an asshole," Grant bit out; the realization that Lane had known she was there settled in and pissed him off.

Gracie didn't say anything, but Grant noticed her chest rising and falling rapidly. Lane's graphic depiction of what happened between them last Friday was turning her on.

"Do you want to watch me kiss him again?" Lane asked Gracie, obviously ignoring Grant completely.

Gracie nodded.

Oh hell. She nodded and Grant had to blink twice to make sure his eyes weren't playing tricks on him.

Lane must've seen it too because he turned toward Grant, his objective written plainly on his ruggedly handsome face.

Grant didn't back down the way he had the last time. He didn't let Lane corner him because he wanted this as much as Lane did. He'd wanted it for a long damn time, but he'd been a coward, afraid of what people would think. It wasn't a secret that Grant wanted Gracie. He'd been chasing after her for years, despite her daddy's warnings.

There would surely be plenty of questions when people realized that Grant wanted both of them, but he couldn't find it in himself to care at the moment because Lane had turned the brunt of his attention on him.

Lane came up to him, his eyes hard, intent. They were almost the same height. Almost. Lane had an inch or two on him and he was bigger, wider. His chest was ripped, his biceps thick, unlike Grant, who was leaner. Not quite as bulky.

"I've been counting down the minutes until I could do this again," Lane whispered, his breath fanning across Grant's face. He smelled like cinnamon. Like the gum he was always chewing.

When Lane's hand cupped his cheek, Grant's breath lodged in his throat.

And then nothing mattered because Lane was kissing him. Hard. Solid. So fucking sweet. And Grant was kissing him back, his hand latching onto Lane's belt buckle and pulling him close so that they were touching from hip to chest.

Lane growled, his hand sliding behind Grant's neck as he held him to him, their tongues sparring as the inferno consumed them. Nothing else mattered right at that moment.

When they came up for air, neither of them turned away immediately, their gazes locked. The silence between them spoke volumes. Regardless of what happened with Gracie, what was happening between the two of them was like a freight train going three hundred miles per hour.

It was right then that Grant realized something.

Whatever this was between them wasn't about to be stopped. They were going to finish this sooner or later.

Grant prayed it was sooner.

CHAPTER FOUR

GRACE COULDN'T BELIEVE WHAT SHE was seeing. Well, no more than she could've believed it the last time she saw these two men kissing. It had been just as intense then as it was now, only they knew she was there this time.

So why wasn't she running for the door?

Nothing made sense at the moment, especially not her reaction to these two men. The fact that they had both kissed her as though they'd been ready to inhale her should've been enough to have her panicking.

She'd kissed both of them. *Both.* Not one. *Two.*

That was twice as many cowboys as she'd kissed in, jeez, it had been close to two years.

And then they'd kissed each other – which they were still doing – the same way which was… Holy crap it was scorching.

When Lane pulled back from Grant, neither man turned to look at her and she practically saw the flames licking at them, ready to pull them under.

"Gracie."

Grace didn't move when Lane said her name. She wasn't sure what she was supposed to do or say, and she wasn't even sure her vocal cords would work. She was stunned silent.

"Does that answer your question?" Lane asked, turning to face her finally.

What question? She'd been asking a question?

Both men moved toward her and Grace realized she was still leaning against the wall where Lane had left her a moment ago.

Still unable to form words, Grace watched as they both invaded her personal space, crowding her with their big bodies, penetrating her with their lust-filled eyes.

"Do you understand yet?" Lane asked.

"Understand what?" she asked, the words little more than a croak.

"We want you," he answered.

"Me?" Gracie cleared her throat. And her mind. This was bullshit is what this was. "*Me?*" she asked again adding another dose of incredulity for good measure. "From the looks of it, y'all want each other. Not me."

"Gorgeous, things aren't always as black and white as you want them to be," Lane offered.

"I don't even know what that means," she told him, glancing over at Grant. The man was looking at her mouth, probably remembering the kiss they'd just shared just a few short minutes ago because Lord knows she remembered it now.

Crap.

"I don't think –"

"*Don't* think," Grant ordered, cutting her off. "Don't try to make sense of it. You never will."

"You're right, I never will. I think the heat has gotten to both of you. You're delusional."

Lane's gaze darted over to Grant's briefly, and Grace couldn't decipher the look that passed between them.

Not that she had time to, because a second later, Lane was kissing her again. And damn it all to hell, she was kissing him back. The hard ridge of his erection was pressing into her belly as she tried to get closer, tried to pull him down to the floor with her because there was no way she could continue to stand up. Her knees were weak.

Heeellllo!

Grace felt Grant behind her. At some point in the last three-point-five seconds, Lane must've turned her because the wall was no longer at her back. Instead, Grant's equally hard body was there, his erection pressing into her lower back while he leaned in and...

Her head was spinning.

Grant's lips were on her neck, Lane's were on her mouth and Lord have mercy, Grace was sandwiched between them. It didn't escape her that she wasn't trying to get away. Not at all.

In fact, she was trying to get closer. To both of them.

One of her hands was gripping Lane's soft hair, the other was clutching Grant's thick thigh, pulling them both against her. And she couldn't stop herself.

Someone was moaning, getting louder as each second passed and when the sound was the only thing filling her head, she realized she was the one moaning. She was practically begging them to get closer although the only way that would be possible was if they were naked and...

Oh, God. What was she doing?

Grace released them both, shoving them away as she darted to the opposite side of the room. Hoping to catch her breath, she placed her palms flat on the kitchen counter, keeping her back to them because there was no way she could look at them. What the hell would they think of her now? She had pushed them off for years until they come knocking on her door and all of a sudden, she was ready to do them both?

Nope. No way. That's not how this was supposed to work.

Grace pushed her hair back from her face as she took a deep breath. *This was too weird.*

"It's not weird," Lane said, and Grace turned to face him.

Had she said that aloud?

"It *is* weird," she assured him. "It's weird and it's not... natural."

Lane laughed, but the sound was gruff and there was no amusement in his dark brown eyes.

"Gracie," Grant called her name and she looked over at him. "Baby."

"Oh, hell no. Don't go and 'baby' me. I'm not your baby. I'm not... I'm not your anything. And the two of you need to leave. We'll pretend this," she twirled her hand around to encompass the three of them, "never happened."

Both men stared at her like she'd gone mad, but Grant was the one who spoke up. "Darlin', that'll never happen. Trust me; I'll never forget this. Not in a million years."

"Well, you're gonna have to try."

☐●☐●☐●☐

GRANT WAS DOING EVERYTHING IN his power to keep at least a few feet between himself and Gracie. And Lane.

The fact that the three of them were in the same room – one that was sealed off to the rest of the world – was more than he had hoped for. At least at this point.

Shit, he was just getting used to the idea of kissing Lane. Now he had the memory of Gracie's lips on his, her hand on his thigh, the fresh scent of her hair, the soft, silky skin of her neck... Yeah, he was in some big trouble here. It had been hard enough to keep from wanting to touch her before now, and now that he'd had even a brief taste of her, he wanted more.

And more.

Hell, he wanted all of her because one taste would never be enough.

But...

As much as Grant didn't want to let go of the moment, he knew they had to take baby steps with her. Gracie wasn't the type of woman who just hopped into bed with any man. Hell, Grant wasn't even sure she wasn't a virgin. Although that bastard she'd dated a few years back had been more than happy to share details of what was supposedly an intimate relationship with the woman.

It was a damn good thing Lane hadn't been around at that time because Grant was pretty sure his friend would've put the asshole six feet under. As it was, Grant had been held back by a couple of the wranglers. And that was the only thing that had saved the bastard at the time.

"I really want you to go," Gracie told them now, her eyes full of emotion.

She was serious.

"We'll go," Grant told her, making his way to her. She didn't back away which was a good sign. "But, baby, this isn't over. I'll give you some space, but... I'm not sure how long I'll be able to stay away."

To his surprise, Gracie didn't argue. The subtle nod of her head looked more like acceptance than anything else. But he knew when to lay off.

"Come on," Grant nodded at Lane, who was standing there staring at them both.

Lane nodded his head, but he didn't speak. His gaze was locked on Gracie and Grant saw, for the first time, such a strong sense of longing in the other man that it made his chest hurt.

Yeah, this wasn't going to be easy. Not on any of them.

When Grant was outside a few minutes later, he stood with his eyes focused on the giant moon. The night was clear and the moon was high, the radiant beam of light shining over the rolling hills that seemed to go on forever.

God he loved it here.

"You okay?" Lane asked as he stepped up beside him, his arm brushing Grant's.

"No," he said truthfully. "I'm not sure I'll ever be okay again."

Lane didn't respond, which was just as well. Grant didn't want to get into why he had suddenly become so sappy. Tonight had been something he'd wanted for as long as he could remember. But kissing Gracie was only the beginning. Taking her to bed was definitely on his mind, but it wasn't the most pressing thing he was thinking about.

No, Grant needed to figure out how this was supposed to work. Between the three of them.

Because he didn't want it any other way.

"I need to head home," Lane finally said.

Grant turned to look at him. He wanted to invite the man back to his cabin, but he knew it was too soon. Especially after what had transpired between them tonight. That kiss... It wasn't just about sex although he had no doubt in his mind that sex with Lane would be off the charts. His dick stirred at the mere thought of Lane naked, pressing up against him while Grant was buried deep inside of him, moaning his name...

Fuck.

"Yeah, I'm thinking about it too," Lane told him, and Grant laughed.

"We can't do this tonight, you know that right?"

"Yeah, I know." Lane sounded incredibly disappointed, but not like Grant was telling him something new.

Lane turned to face him and Grant couldn't keep from looking into his eyes. Goddamn the man was handsome. Big and broad, he almost made Grant feel small although six-foot-one was not small by any stretch of the imagination. But it wasn't just Lane's physical presence that made him so big. It was the life in him.

"I'd give anything to be back inside her house, to have you both up next to me, Grant. I don't want this to fade away. Do you understand?" Lane was serious. Deadly serious. "I've wanted this for so long. Both of you. And goddammit, I've tried to figure out what it would be like with just one, not both of you, but it doesn't work. Well, it does and it doesn't." Lane smiled sheepishly.

"I know," Grant whispered back.

They stood there like that for a few minutes, neither of them talking.

"I'll see you tomorrow," Lane finally said as he reached out and touched Grant's hand. From the outside, it would've looked innocent, but being this close to Lane, Grant saw the hunger and longing in the man's beautiful brown eyes.

"Tomorrow," Grant agreed.

Unable to make his feet move, Grant stood there in the yard surrounding Gracie's cabin as he watched Lane walk away.

When Lane was out of sight, Grant turned to look back at Gracie's house. He was surprised to see her standing there, framed by the doorjamb of the front door. Before he could say anything, she took a step back and the door closed slowly. She'd heard everything they said and she hadn't run, hadn't shut the door on them. She had stood there listening. And Grant was inclined to believe she was on the same page they were. It wouldn't be long.

He hoped.

CHAPTER FIVE

"SO, HOW'S GRANT?" FAITH ASKED the following Friday night while the two of them were sitting in the main recreation room keeping an eye on things.

Out of the five of them, Grace and her four sisters took alternate shifts hanging out with the guests on Friday and Saturday nights. She would have to admit that it usually wasn't a hardship because with as many guests as they saw in a given week, there was never a lull. And tonight was no exception.

"Shut up," Grace mumbled through gritted teeth as she pretended to be watching the few groups scattered throughout the two-thousand square foot recreation area. For the past week, Faith had been giving her shit about Grant, and Grace's patience with her sister had finally run out. *"Out of condoms yet?" "Who's the chocolate syrup for? You or him?" "I thought I heard someone screaming his name the other night. Was that you?"*

No matter what Grace did, she couldn't get Faith to shut up. The only positive was that, as far as she could tell, Faith hadn't run her big mouth to their sisters or to their father. And yes, that was the only positive in the entire screwed up situation.

Not only had Faith been reminding her of Grant, which in turn reminded her of Lane, but Grace had also been thinking about them far too much. When she was awake, she couldn't stop thinking about the kisses they shared. When she was asleep, things got significantly hotter until she was waking up soaked in sweat, completely frustrated.

Both men had given her a wide berth for the better part of the week. Although they both checked on her each morning, neither of them were pushing her. For anything. And that disappointed her, even if she didn't want to admit it.

No, what Grace wanted was to go back to Monday night when the three of them were standing in her living room and insist that they explain how this was possible. People didn't have three-way relationships. Did they? God, she didn't know and she damn sure didn't want to look on the internet to find out because heaven only knew what she'd find.

"Faith."

Grace looked up at the same time her sister did. There, on the other side of the room was Rusty Ashmore. Glancing back to her sister, Grace noticed that Faith was blushing profusely, but she wasn't smiling.

"Uh-oh," Grace muttered beneath her breath, an impish grin tipping her lips. Payback was a bitch.

It was Faith's turn to tell Grace to shut up.

She didn't because what fun would that be.

"Hey, Rusty," Grace greeted him as he moved closer, his eyes glued to Faith. "How's it hangin'?"

"Grace," he said in response, seemingly ignoring her entirely. Grace laughed.

"Well, you two kids have fun. Oh, and if you need any, I seem to have an abundance of chocolate syrup that I won't be needing," she offered to the pair as she pushed out of her chair and headed across the room.

A quick peek back and Grace grinned at her sister's bewildered expression. Nope, she hadn't expected that one.

Just when she was going to try to sneak out, Grace skimmed the room before her gaze landed on two men at the pool table, both of them laughing.

Grant and Lane.

Unable to stop herself, Grace stared at them, watching the easy way they talked and laughed with one another. Maybe she never noticed it before, probably because she had no reason to, but it was clear by their body language that they found one another attractive. She doubted anyone else would see it because as far as the rest of the world was concerned, they were just two friends who liked to rib each other constantly.

God, they were incredibly attractive. Lane's booming laugh echoed in the room, causing several of the female guests to glance his direction. A pang of jealousy resounded in her chest and Grace immediately pushed it aside. She didn't care what they did. Or with who they did it with.

Liar.

As though they felt her observing them, they both turned at the exact same time. Grace instantly turned away, but she didn't run for the door as she had originally intended. No, there was some sort of centrifugal force pulling her back and she didn't try to fight it.

She didn't want to.

And that meant she'd gone completely crazy.

"Gracie!"

This time Grace turned to see her sister Mercy coming her way and that alone should've sent her screaming from the building. At least one time or another, Grace had wondered how she came about her name because the one thing Mercy lacked was, well, mercy. She should've hightailed it out the door, but thanks to the odd magnetic pull from the two men across the room, she couldn't get her feet to move.

"Where've you been?" Mercy asked as she approached.

"Here," she said, confused.

"I've been looking all over for you."

"Me?"

"No, the dude standing behind you. Yes, you. Shit."

Ummm… okay. Grace stared back at Mercy, waiting for her sister to continue.

"I need to run into town tomorrow. I was wondering if you had a list of things you wanted me to get for you."

Grace's mouth fell open and her ears began to burn. At that same moment, Mercy grinned like a fool. "No? Nothing. Fine. I'll go ask Grant if he needs anything from town."

Grace grabbed her sister's arm just when she started to turn away. "Don't you dare!"

Mercy laughed and heads began to turn.

"Relax, sister mine. I won't say anything. At least not yet."

"What does that mean?" God, Grace could feel the blackmail coming on.

"It means that if you go over there and talk to those two cowboys, I'll keep my mouth shut. If you don't… Well, I'm gonna have a little fun." Mercy made a spectacle of looking around the room, causing Grace to look, as well.

Shit. There were way too many employees, not to mention guests, in the rec room at the moment which meant if Mercy opened her big mouth, Grace wouldn't be able to show her face for at least a decade. Maybe two.

"Fine," Grace said in a harsh whisper. "I'll go over there. You better keep your damn mouth shut."

"Wait. Where're you goin'?" Mercy asked when Grace turned to walk away.

"I've got a sister to pummel into the ground first. But then, as I said, I'll go talk to them."

With that, Grace stormed away to the sound of Mercy laughing her ass off behind her.

□●□●□●□

"GRACIE DOESN'T LOOK HAPPY," LANE mentioned as he lined up to take his shot at the table.

Grant didn't turn to look. Instead, he tipped his beer back and watched Lane over the edge of the bottle. He knew Gracie didn't look happy. She hadn't looked happy since the night they'd kissed her.

In fact, for most of the week she had managed to evade them at every turn. They'd run into her a few times, but she'd been overly polite, refusing to make eye contact which had begun to piss him off.

And right now, Grant wasn't in the mood to watch her walk away.

Hell, he was getting a little tired of the whole scene, but he had promised Lane that he'd come to the rec center for an hour or two. Glancing up at the clock on the wall, he was glad to see that his two hours were almost up.

"Shit," Lane mumbled when he missed, his eyes transfixed on something behind Grant. "Mercy's on her way over."

Yep, *shit* was right.

Grant stood up straight, downing what was left of his beer when she reached his side.

"I've just handed you the winning cards. If you don't know how to play this hand, then y'all are sad, sad excuses for men." With that, the blonde walked right on by.

Grant looked at Lane, his eyebrows raised in question but his friend didn't have an answer either.

"Can I play?"

It was a damn good thing his beer was empty because Grant would've spilled its entire contents down his shirt. A small glance to his left assured him that yes, he'd heard correctly. Gracie was standing at his side, peering up at him as she waited for him to answer.

"Sure."

"Man, we're in the middle of a game," Lane huffed, grinning from ear to ear.

"I'll play the winner."

Grant glanced down at the table, counting the balls and trying to figure out the odds of him winning. Slim to none, and the wicked grin on Lane's face said he knew it, too.

"Good idea," Lane said as he moved closer, brushing against Gracie as he passed by. "She'll play the winner. Oh, wait. It's still my turn."

Lane strolled back to the table, his cocky walk exaggerated as he all but celebrated his success.

Then again, unless the guy fucked up majorly, there wasn't a chance in hell that Grant was going to win this one anyway. He was a good pool player, but he wasn't great. And tonight he was completely off his game. More so now that Gracie was close enough that he could smell the fruity scent of her shampoo.

"You're losing," Grace told him, a smirk on her pretty mouth.

"I am," he agreed. No reason to deny it, the truth was laid out right there on the table for all to see.

Laid out on the table…

Lord, his mind was going in a direction that it really shouldn't but no matter how hard he tried, Grant couldn't reel it back in.

"Are you doing all right?" he asked, trying to make small talk.

"Nope, but I'm here. That's all that matters."

Grant shifted so he could look at Gracie directly. "What does that mean?"

"It means I'm being blackmailed by my sister," Gracie answered easily, still watching Lane. "All thanks to you."

Grant glanced around the room until he located not one but all four of Gracie's sisters. Faith, who was currently chatting it up with Rusty and looking none too happy about it; Trinity, who was sitting on a chair with a book open in her lap; Hope, who was sitting at a small table with two other women, laughing openly about something one woman said; and... Yep, there was the troublemaker. Mercy. Although Grant had no idea what she could possibly have on Gracie.

"Faith's blackmailing you?" he asked, stunned. Little Faith Lambert was nothing if not sweet and seemingly innocent. She was the youngest of the five sisters, but that didn't necessarily mean anything.

"Nope. She went and delegated that to Mercy."

"She told..."

"Yep. Are you happy now?"

It was clear that Gracie certainly wasn't happy, but he didn't get a chance to answer when Lane walked up and clapped him on the back. Hard. "Maybe next time."

Shit. Looking at the pool table, Grant noticed that Lane had certainly swept him.

"My turn?" Gracie asked sweetly, but again, she didn't meet his eyes.

"Looks like it." Grant handed her the pool stick he'd been using and took a step back so he could watch the pair.

It looked like it was going to be one of those nights.

□●□●□●□

LANE HADN'T HEARD THE CONVERSATION between Grant and Gracie, but he didn't have to be a brainiac to figure out that Gracie wasn't happy about something.

"You break," Lane told Gracie as he once again brushed up against her as he passed by.

Gracie nodded, paying special attention to the chalk in her hand. He knew she wasn't that worried about this game, so he figured she was just trying to avoid looking at him.

Several minutes later, Lane had gone easy on her to avoid ending the game too soon. It was clear that pool wasn't one of Gracie's favorite things to do, but she was there, and that was all that really mattered to him. She and Grant. His night had gone from good to phenomenal when she approached. And now he didn't want it to end.

"S'up?" Cody Mercer, Dead Heat Ranch's head equipment mechanic, said as he approached, his eyes darting between the three of them before landing back on Lane.

Fuck. Shit. Damn.

"Nada," he told Cody. "What's up with you? How's your mama?"

"Good, man," Cody answered, staring back at Lane as he sipped his beer.

Lane liked Cody. He was a good guy. But at the moment, his presence meant Lane's night was about to go to shit even if Cody didn't mean for it to. The guy had good intentions, but it wasn't a secret that he opened his mouth at the most inopportune times. Right now was one of them.

"She just got out of the hospital," Cody declared, looking over at Gracie. "So who–"

"They find out what was wrong with her?" Lane asked, purposely cutting Cody off, trying to tell him no with his eyes. *Do not go there, bro. That's not gonna be cool.*

"Dehydration," Cody said easily. "She had the flu and she was so dehydrated, her blood pressure dropped. They filled her full of fluids. All's good now."

Maybe all was good with Cody's mom, but it wasn't going to be good if the man shot off at the mouth. Lane didn't say as much.

"Good to hear."

"Your turn," Gracie called to him as she stepped back from the table.

Lane was hesitant to move away from Cody, wanting to be close enough to tackle him if he said what Lane expected him to say. But, he didn't want to look suspicious, so he moved over to the table, opposite Gracie.

"So," Cody began, and Lane closed his eyes, "which one of you lucky bastards won the bet?"

Lane lined up a shot, took it. The balls clanked together from the force of the hit, but he sank his ball and then turned to look at Grant.

"What bet?" Gracie asked, her eyes on Cody.

"The one these two've had going for... How long's it been now? Two years?"

Gracie looked more than a little interested and when Grant tried to step in front of her, blocking her view of Cody, she pushed him aside. Sort of. She tried to push him aside, but Grant held his ground so she just moved around him.

"Two years, huh?" Gracie asked, pretending not to be in the dark. "That long? Wow. I had no idea."

"Shit yeah," Cody laughed. "I thought for sure they'd never get you to give in to either of them. So which is it? Who gets to claim this as a date?"

CHAPTER SIX

GRACIE COULD FEEL STEAM COMING out of her ears.

A bet?

For the first time that night, she met Grant's navy blue gaze, hoping like hell she wouldn't see what she expected to see. But, sure enough, there it was. Guilt.

"You're a bastard," she whispered, handing him the pool stick as she walked as calmly as she could manage passed him.

"Gracie, wait," Lane hollered.

Grace didn't stop. She couldn't. They'd made a fucking bet which went to prove that the other night had just been bullshit. They had made a fool out of her, playing her like an idiot. All so that one of them could win some stupid fucking bet.

She had just rounded the side of the building, grateful for the shadows that would hopefully conceal her misery because the tears were right there, threatening to fall.

"Goddammit, Gracie, wait."

She was just about to up her pace when a strong hand came down on her arm, stopping her. Rather than turning to face him, Grace kept her eyes forward, counting down from one hundred to keep the tears at bay. It was stupid of her to cry anyway. It wasn't like she had a relationship with either of them. They'd kissed her. That was all. Hell, they had kissed each other, so it clearly meant little to them.

"Look at me," Grant's voice was low and deep, an urgent plea in his tone.

"I can't," she told him honestly. If she did, she'd surely cry, and she damn sure wasn't going to let him know his deceit had hurt her so much.

Grant startled her when his body heat enveloped her, his hard body against her back, his heavy arms coming around her gently. "Let us explain."

Us?

As though she'd welcomed him with open arms, Lane moved around to stand in front of her, efficiently sandwiching her between the two of them. Great. This definitely wasn't helping.

"Yes, we made a bet. Two years ago. It was stupid," Grant explained.

"Stupid, maybe. But it wasn't bad, Gracie," Lane explained.

"So who won?" she asked, feeling foolish.

"Neither of us," Grant said, his voice soft against her ear. "There is no winner here. Especially if you walk away."

"What am I supposed to do?" she asked dubiously. "I'm not your play toy," she told them both. "You should know me better than that."

Grant's arms loosened, but only enough so that he could turn her around to face him. He was standing much too close. So close that Grace had to look up into his eyes.

"The bet was inconsequential, Gracie. It meant nothing. You are what we want, what–"

"We?" she exclaimed. "Are you still on this kick? What the hell does 'we' mean, Grant? There can't be a 'we'. It doesn't work that way."

"It can work that way," he said softly, his finger and thumb now gripping her chin gently. So gently, Grace felt the tears rush forward.

"This doesn't make sense."

Lane stepped forward, closer to Grace's back, shielding them all with his big body. At least that's what it would look like for someone passing by.

"One chance, Gracie," Lane pleaded. "Let us show you."

Grant leaned forward, pressing his lips to hers lightly, and Grace was so tempted to give in. His mouth was warm and surprisingly soft. It was just like the other night all over again. She wanted to feel his arms around her, to feel his body against hers, his lips, his tongue.

But she couldn't. Because Lane was there.

And damn it, she wanted him too and it just didn't make sense. How could she want them both? And they both want her? And each other?

It was too damned confusing.

Grace pushed against Grant's solid chest, and to her surprise, he stepped back.

"Leave me alone," she begged and then slipped out from between them. "If you don't want to hurt me, you'll stop this game right now."

Grant and Lane were both watching her. She could hardly make out their expressions in the shadows, but she could feel the heat coming off them. They wanted sex. That was all.

"You've got each other," she said, just before she turned and... ran.

□●□●□●□

GRANT WATCHED GRACIE WALK AWAY. Well, run was more like it. Yeah, the hot little cowgirl was running full out, like the hounds of hell were on her ass.

"We need to go after her," Lane said absently, still standing beside Grant.

"Yep," he agreed.

Neither of them moved.

"What happens when she doesn't open the door?" Lane asked.

"No idea," Grant offered.

"How 'bout I lead the way?"

"All right."

Grant didn't stop watching Gracie until she was completely out of sight. His feet wanted him to move, but his heart was lodged in his throat. He couldn't fuck this up. Not after what had occurred between them the last time they went to her house.

"Come on," Lane encouraged, finally taking a step forward. Then another.

Grant fell into step with him and before he knew it, they were taking the steps up to Gracie's little cabin that looked like so many of the others on the outside, including his own.

Lane knocked on the door, but there was no answer.

"She's not gonna answer," Lane stated unnecessarily.

Grant reached for the doorknob, figuring what the hell. He was shocked when the knob turned easily and the door opened.

"Gracie," he called, stepping inside because no, he was not going to let this opportunity pass him by.

"Go away." Her voice was muffled, and that was when Grant noticed she was lying on the couch, a pillow covering her face.

Grant glanced back at Lane and the other man shut the door. Locked it.

The click of the deadbolt got Gracie's attention because she lifted the pillow enough to peek out, but then she promptly put it back in place. "I don't have anything to say to you. Either of you."

Lane being Lane walked right over to the couch, lifted Gracie's legs and plopped down before resting her booted feet on his lap.

"What are you doing?" she shouted, shooting up to a sitting position which gave Grant the opportunity he needed.

He took a seat where her head had just been, then pulled her back down so that her head was propped on his thigh.

"Y'all are impossible, you know that?"

"Oh, gorgeous, there're plenty of possibilities where we're concerned."

Grant laughed at Lane's garbled words. He clearly hadn't been intending for them to hear him.

Unable to resist, Grant slid his fingers through Gracie's shiny gold hair. Her eyes widened as she stared up at him. "What are you doing?" she asked again, this time her voice was soft.

"What does it look like?" he asked, continuing to brush his fingers through her long, silky tresses.

Gracie nearly came off the couch, her attention turning to Lane once more. "What the hell are *you* doing?"

"I'm takin' off your boots. What does it look like?"

"Why the hell are you doin' that?" she squealed as she tried to pull her leg back.

"They kinda get in the way," he told her directly, again making Grant laugh.

When she looked back at him, he couldn't hide his amusement. "Sorry. You can leave 'em on if you want. Boots are optional."

"Oh. My. God." The exasperation in her tone dripped from every word, but Grant was pretty sure he saw a small smile turn the very corners of her lips.

Gracie flopped back down, and Grant had to shift to avoid some serious damage to the family jewels.

No one said a word while Grant continued to stroke her hair and Lane finally managed to remove both of her boots, tossing them onto the floor. Gracie was watching them both, her eyes darting from one to the other as though she were going to be able to predict what came next. And if Grant had to guess, she assumed they were just going to jump on her like dogs in heat.

They didn't.

Grant used his fingertips to massage her scalp while Lane slipped her socks off and then began to rub her bare feet.

"This isn't fair," she muttered.

"What's not fair?" Grant asked.

"Y'all are seducing me."

"Is it working?"

"No." Gracie sighed and her eyes closed.

"Looks like it's working to me," Lane offered.

They both peered at one another when Gracie didn't argue.

There was so much heat in that one look, Grant was surprised he didn't spontaneously combust.

This was going to happen. And it was going to happen tonight. Right here.

Part of him was anxious. Another part was scared.

But only because he feared that what they were about to do was going to change all three of them forever.

□●□●□●□

LANE HAD BEEN WITH PLENTY of women. He'd also been with plenty of men.

Never once had any of those situations felt remotely similar to this.

He was nervous.

That was new.

He was also a little reticent.

Only because what he assumed was about to happen was going to change his life irrevocably.

There would be no turning back. Not for him.

Part of it was due to the fact that he was already a little bit in love with both of them. Had been for quite a while although he hadn't admitted it. Hadn't had any reason to. Until now.

Lane continued to massage Gracie's small, delicate feet. They were soft and her toenails were painted a shiny blue which suited her perfectly. He'd always thought she was tough on the outside but fun and flirty underneath it all, even if she didn't let many people see that side of her.

As he continued to move his hands just a little higher, rubbing her ankles, he circled her bare calves, his eyes sliding up her toned legs, stopping at the frayed hem of her short jean shorts. He loved these shorts. Fucking loved them. By the time he was at her knees, Gracie was moaning softly. Lane looked up her slim body to see that Grant had also ventured to other parts. He was methodically rubbing her chest, just above her pert little breasts. Gracie's ribcage was rising more rapidly now, her body bowing every time Grant started to move a little lower.

"Please don't stop," Gracie whispered, surprising them both.

Hoping she was talking to Grant, Lane released her feet, shifting so he could ease out from beneath her legs. Without leaving the couch, he managed to place one knee between her legs as he moved over her. Her eyes were bright and clear as she stared up at him, Grant's hand wandering just a little lower until he was cupping her breast through her shirt.

"I'm gonna kiss you, Gracie." He said the words and paused momentarily so she would have a chance to tell him no. If she did, he'd back off and wouldn't push. If she didn't, he was going to kiss her. And he probably wasn't going to stop until she was naked.

She didn't say no and she didn't say yes. She didn't say anything at all, but Gracie did nod her head. It was nearly imperceptible, but Lane was watching her closely, praying she wouldn't push him away.

With one hand on the back of the couch, the other planted on the cushion just above her shoulder, Lane held himself above her while he brushed his lips over hers gently.

And that's when the fire erupted.

Gracie reached for him, pulling him hard enough to throw him off balance. Lane managed to catch himself, scared he was going to crush her. But then all fear dissipated, the only thing that was left was her tongue in his mouth and Grant's hand in his hair.

He growled, unable to control himself. They were both touching him and he thought for sure he was going to go up in flames. It was everything he'd ever wanted and it was more than he expected.

The kiss continued for longer than he had originally planned and when they both pulled back, they were breathless, staring back at one another. Gracie's eyes were the first to stray, and she was looking up at Grant, which caused Lane to do the same. When he did, he realized just how close they were. Hovering above Gracie on one hand, Lane used his other to grip the back of Grant's neck, pulling him close until their mouths crashed together.

He was growling again. Or maybe that was Grant. He wasn't quite sure, and he really didn't care because Gracie had pulled his shirt free from his jeans and she was working on his belt buckle which made him realize... Fuck. He didn't know what he realized, but he knew he needed to stop. It was the right thing to do.

For now.

He couldn't break free from the kiss because Grant tasted too damn good. And Grant kissed him back as though he was starving for him, the same way Lane had been all week.

But he knew he had to stop. He had to.

Or shit, it would be over long before it started.

CHAPTER SEVEN

GRACE KNEW SHE WASN'T THINKING clearly. She had accepted that fact the moment they put their hands on her.

But unlike the other night, her good sense had taken a midnight ride right out the door and here she was eager and willing to get close to both of these men. Closer than she ever imagined she would with just one of them, much less both of them.

But there it was. A simple, yet very complicated, fact. Something she could no longer deny.

They said this type of... Did they call this a relationship? No. She was probably getting ahead of herself by assuming too much. Not that it mattered. She was taking Grant and Lane at their word that this type of *relationship* – for lack of a better word – was possible, and despite the fact that she had no idea how it actually worked, she was going to trust them.

Or maybe she just trusted her hormones.

One way or the other, Grace was going to see where this went. And if her good sense returned by morning, she'd deal with the repercussions at that time. For now... For now, she just wanted them.

"God, that's hot," she whispered, surprising herself when she spoke aloud.

Grant and Lane pulled back from one another just a little, and Grace immediately wished she could watch them some more. Or participate. Yes, participate would be good.

The next thing she knew, she was a willing and active participant because Lane's mouth was on hers again, but his hand was snaking between their bodies as he grabbed both of her wrists. She'd been attempting to undo his pants and when she tried again, he laughed, his chuckle reverberating inside of her mouth, making her laugh, too.

"Not yet, sweetness. Too much too soon and I'll be out of commission long before I'm ready," he told her with a grin the size of Texas on his extremely handsome face.

"Help her sit up," Grant instructed, clearly talking to Lane.

Lane got to his feet in a rush, and, with ease, he took her hands and pulled her up until she was standing right in front of him. Grace knew she should've been appalled at her behavior, but she couldn't seem to find it in her to care. It was like she was at a buffet after spending an eternity without food. She wanted it all and she wanted it right now.

Obviously realizing she was ready to get on with it, Lane eliminated the space between them as he leaned down to claim her mouth once more. Her hands immediately went around him while his came down to cup her butt, pulling her against him.

He was hard. Everywhere.

As she got lost in Lane's kisses again, another hard body came up behind her and she wished she could turn around and kiss Grant at the same time. But she couldn't seem to break away from Lane and not because he was holding on to her. No, she seemed to be the aggressor at the moment which was so completely unlike her, she wondered if maybe she'd hit her head.

Grant's mouth was on her neck. Hot and so, so soft. She released Lane's hair so she could reach behind her, grabbing hold of Grant's head and pulling him closer. Somewhere along the way, they'd both ditched their hats and she had no idea when that happened, nor did she care. The only thing she could think about was the fact that they had on too many clothes.

A firm hand snaked between her body and Lane's, and she had no idea whose it was, but she didn't care. Whoever it was began unbuttoning her shirt and she wanted to help him along because she needed to get closer, to feel the heat of their bodies against hers. And they weren't going fast enough as far as she was concerned.

When Lane's mouth broke free from hers, Grace whimpered, hoping they'd find encouragement in her elusive plea.

"You're making me crazy, Gracie," Lane whispered, his head coming down until his forehead rested against hers. "I need to feel both of you."

Yes. That's exactly what she was thinking.

"We need to get more comfortable," Lane mumbled, and Grace realized what he was requesting.

Grace's gaze slid toward the bedroom door just as Grant pulled her shirt open. Releasing her grip, which was still tightly twined on Grant's head behind her, she allowed him to slide the cotton down her arms until it was a mere memory on the floor at their feet.

"Bedroom," she whispered, turning her head so she could see Grant. He leaned in and kissed her, his mouth warm and soft against hers and she immediately wanted more of him. In a flash, she spun around, her arms wrapping around Grant's neck as she tried to form her body to his. He lifted her with ease and she wrapped her legs around his waist, their mouths fused as one.

How he managed, she had no idea, but the next thing she knew, they were in her bedroom and she was back on her feet, pressed up against Grant's hard body while Lane was at Grant's back. They were sandwiching him between them, and Grace found it difficult to focus on anything but watching as Lane leaned in and pressed his mouth to Grant's neck.

For whatever reason, Grace had never considered the overwhelming heat of watching two men together but ever since that night she watched them in Grant's kitchen, she found herself frequently replaying the scene. And now they were giving her a front row seat to a superbly erotic show once again.

Grant's head fell back on his shoulders, but his hands never left Grace's body. He was skimming them over her torso, up over her breasts and she wished she were naked, wanting to feel the rough rasp of his fingers against her nipples.

Reaching around behind her, she quickly unclasped her bra and tossed it aside before working to free the buttons on Grant's shirt while she continued to watch the two men. They were beautiful. Dark hair, bronzed skin covering all that hard muscle, and a longing heat in their eyes that spoke to her on so many levels. She was pretty sure she could've been content watching them.

But joining in was much more fun.

"I need you naked," Grant mumbled as he lifted his head and opened his eyes, pinning her with a dazed look. "Both of you."

"What are you waiting for?" Lane asked, grinning.

"I just have one question," Grace stated, and both men stopped moving, giving her their full attention.

□●□●□●□

GRANT WASN'T ABOUT TO PANIC, but he was watching Gracie carefully.

Her eyes roamed from his face, slowly down over his body and then back up. He held his breath, waiting to hear what she had to say.

"Are boots still optional?" she asked deadpan, and Grant nearly swallowed his tongue.

Laughing, Lane moved around to where Gracie stood. Wrapping his thick arms around her, he lifted her and tossed her onto her bed, coming down on top of her, boots and all.

"Do you want us to keep our boots on, baby? Cuz I'm good with that," Lane teased.

Grant wasn't leaving his boots on, dammit. In less than two minutes, he was naked and in desperate need of touching one or both of them in the next few seconds.

He managed to shove Lane off Gracie playfully, scooping her up into his arms and pulling her on top of him. "I prefer no boots," he told her. "At least this time. There'll be plenty of opportunities for experimentation later."

Gracie's eyebrows shot up and Grant lifted his head to meet her mouth before she could say anything. She tasted sweet and spicy, and Grant loved the feel of her warm, smooth skin against his hands. He trailed them over her back, down over her flawless rounded ass until he landed on her smooth, silky thighs. He worked his way back up, but Gracie lifted her hips and he realized what she was requesting.

With ease, he slid his hands between them and quickly unhooked the button on her shorts. She was naked from the waist up, but Lane was already working on getting her all the way there. The man had shed his own clothes in record time too and was working to slide her shorts down her hips.

Grant repositioned when Gracie did, holding her tightly against him when Lane relieved her of her shorts. Grant locked his lips with hers, his hands finding her pert breasts as she moaned into his mouth. She was hot and sweet, her soft skin pressed against him everywhere.

Heaven.

When the bed dipped from Lane's weight, Grant moved again, offering him as much room as possible. In doing so, Gracie turned, meeting Lane's mouth with her own while Grant trailed his lips down her neck, inhaling the sweet sexy scent of her skin as he left a trail heading south.

With Lane perched beside them, they were a jumble of hands and mouths as they trailed kisses along Gracie's sexy little body, and Grant had to wonder whether Lane was having as difficult a time restraining himself as he was. God, she made him ache for her. And it didn't help that Lane, in all of his naked glory, was brushing up against him, their legs scraping against one another, Lane's hands drifting lazily over his skin every so often.

"Don't move," Lane demanded, his head lifting enough that their eyes met.

Grant didn't have to wonder who he was talking to because his dark gaze was locked on Grant's face.

It was then that Lane disappeared, but he didn't go far. Grant couldn't see him because Gracie was still on top of him, her thighs gripping his hips as he fondled her breast, rolling her nipple between his thumb and forefinger.

"Does it feel good?" he asked.

"Yes," she said on a sigh.

When he pulled her up his body so that he could reach her breast with his mouth, Grant thought for a brief second that he was going to lose it. Lane's hands rested on his thighs, and Grant waited for what would come next.

"Yes!" Gracie moaned loudly, her head falling back, her chest thrusting forward. Grant took advantage of the opportunity, sucking her nipple into his mouth while his hands roamed down her back to her ass. On instinct, he gripped her soft flesh, pulling her butt cheeks apart to give Lane a better view of what he imagined was the sweetest pussy they'd ever know.

"Fuck. You're wet, baby," Lane growled from the end of the bed. "So wet."

Grant was suddenly jealous that he wasn't able to see what Lane was doing. As it was, he could feel Lane's hand every so often along the hard ridge of his cock. But the man didn't stop to play with him; he simply continued to torment Gracie while he gave them a play by play.

"Fuck, baby, you're tight. Do you like that? Oh, yeah. Two fingers."

"Oh, God," Gracie cried out. "Don't stop, Lane. Oh, don't stop."

"Aww, damn. You like to be finger fucked, don't you, baby? Do you want to come for us?"

"Yes, yes. God, yes."

Gracie was thrusting back against Lane, and Grant had no choice but to release her breast while he watched her. She was perched above him; her head tipped back, the smooth column of her neck made his mouth water with the need to taste her there. Her neck was sensitive; he'd already realized that the last time they'd been here.

"I've gotta taste you," Lane said, but Grant doubted Gracie heard him. Her body thrashed against him, and when Lane leaned forward, his weight pressing against Grant's thighs, Grant was surprised she didn't come up off the bed.

"Fuck," Grant groaned. Yeah, he hadn't thought this all the way through. If he didn't get a grip on himself, he was going to end this – at least his part in this – before it ever got started.

And that would be a total shame.

Because now Lane's mouth was on his cock and he wasn't shy about it either.

And just like the last time, his wicked tongue sent Grant spiraling into orbit.

"Fuck, oh, fuck," he mumbled over and over, his eyes rolling back in his head as the pleasure accosted him.

Gracie shifted off him, leaving Grant free to look down the length of his body to see Lane bent down between Grant's legs. His cock was deep in Lane's blissfully hot mouth and he was scared he was going to come before he was ready.

"So good," he growled, reaching down to grab hold of Lane's hair. "Don't make me come, dammit."

"You taste good," Lane told him when he let Grant slip from his mouth. But then, thankfully, Lane's attention was diverted to Gracie, which gave Grant a moment to breathe. A moment to rein himself in.

"Come here, baby. I want to taste you now."

Grant assisted by reaching for Gracie, pulling her on top of him again, but this time he had her on her back above him.

"Fuck yes," Lane groaned. "This is like fucking heaven."

And that was the moment Grant learned exactly what Lane meant.

□●□●□●□

LANE WAS PRETTY SURE HE'D died and gone to heaven. The only thing that could've possibly been better would've been if they were on a beach somewhere. Then again, the sand wouldn't have been conducive for what he had planned, so no... Nothing could've been better than this.

With Gracie sprawled on top of Grant, Lane had a smorgasbord laid out in front of him, and he found his hands were shaking with the need that coursed through his veins. Forcing Grant's legs farther apart, Lane crawled up onto the bed once again, trying to get comfortable. As he leaned forward, he brushed his fingers through the soft curls between Gracie's legs before separating her pussy lips and exposing her to his gaze. Her body tensed slightly as she tried to get closer to his mouth.

Huffing out a laugh, Lane leaned in and slid his tongue through her soft, wet folds. He lapped at her gently, slowly, unwilling to rush because he'd been waiting for this moment for as long as he could remember. Shifting, he managed to free one hand, using one to hold her lips open as he teased her clit and the other to stroke Grant's heavily veined cock. He was silky-smooth between his fingers.

"Lane," Gracie moaned. "More. I need more."

Lane obliged, thrusting his tongue into her pussy while he continued to stroke Grant slowly. He worked them both while his own need blossomed into a full-blown wildfire burning inside of him. He wanted to thrust himself inside of Gracie. At the same time, he wanted to feel Grant's big cock in his ass.

Oh, fuck. If he kept up that cerebral visual aid, he was going to come without either of them touching him.

The next thing he knew, Gracie was sitting up, pulling him by the hair and they were moving. He didn't have time to object – not that he would have – before he found himself on his back, this time Grant between his thighs, sucking his cock deep in his mouth in an abrupt move that stole the air from Lane's lungs.

"Fuck!" Lane roared, but the sound was muffled when Gracie crushed her mouth to his. He did the only thing he knew to do; he reached for her. His hands had a mind of their own as he felt her up, everywhere. The kiss detonated, and he quite literally saw stars as Grant's wicked mouth pushed him closer and closer to the edge.

When it became too much, Lane broke the kiss, looking up at Gracie. "Sit on my face, baby."

She looked at him sideways, but then he grabbed her waist, urging her up his body until – thank you, God – she was straddling his head. In order to keep his focus off the mind blowing blowjob that Grant was giving him, Lane shoved his face between Gracie's thighs and lapped her cunt like a starving man.

There was a brief reprieve while Lane focused all of his attention on eating Gracie's pussy, but then Grant threw him for a loop when he buried his finger into Lane's ass. Lane dug his head into the bed as he cried out, the sensation so fucking good, he was scared he came without even realizing it.

"You like that?" Grant asked, his deep voice sliding over him, pulling him back from the brink momentarily.

He realized Gracie had moved and she was no longer perched above him, obstructing his view of the man who was now finger fucking his ass. Another finger joined the first and Lane bent his knees, encouraging Grant to go deeper while he reached for Gracie, needing to touch her still. "Fuck me," he begged. "Oh, hell, Grant. Fuck me hard."

"I plan to," Grant told him but the blissful friction of his fingers in his ass disappeared far too soon.

Lane fought to catch his breath as he watched Grant move across the room. He was reaching for his jeans and Lane thought for a second that he was going to die. If Grant left, he'd lose it.

But Grant wasn't leaving. He tossed something toward Gracie, who caught it with a laugh. And then she was between his legs, working a condom over his throbbing shaft while Grant suited up.

Once they were all three properly protected, Gracie crawled over Lane. When she leaned forward, he wrapped his arms around her and flipped their positions so that she was on her back and he was above her.

"I've wanted you for so long," he mumbled in a faint whisper, fearful that he was about to say too much. "So long, Gracie."

"You've got me," she told him. "You've got us both."

Yes, he did. And he wasn't even going to try to figure out when he'd become the luckiest bastard in the world because right now he was in possession of the title and he fully intended to be the reigning champ for all of eternity.

At least he hoped.

Lane eased himself between Gracie's legs until his cock lined up with the heated entrance to her pussy. The urgency that rolled through him damn near had him slamming into her. But at the last possible second, he remembered who he was with. He wanted to be gentle with her. To take it slow. To savor the moment.

"Fuck me, Lane," Gracie bit out as her hips drove upward, forcing him to sink inside of her.

"Oh, hell," he growled as her heat engulfed him. He stilled inside of her as he slid farther, deeper.

"Yes," she hissed. "You feel so good."

When he was lodged to the hilt inside of her, the bed dipped behind him and that familiar tingle started at the base of his spine. He bit his bottom lip – hard – in an attempt to stave off his release. He knew what was coming and couldn't wait much longer. He was so amped up; just the thought of Grant was threatening to send him into oblivion.

Something cool ran down the crack of his ass and he peered over his shoulder to see Grant with a small packet of lube. *Where the hell had that come from?*

"Optimism, baby. I've always been optimistic," Grant said as though he'd read Lane's mind. Or maybe Lane had said the words aloud. He didn't know. Didn't care.

Because that was when the world tilted on its axis as Grant slid into his body. Lane held his breath as he pushed back slightly, forcing Grant deeper.

Gracie's legs came up and wrapped around his hips, holding him to her and that was a good thing because Lane was suddenly overwhelmed with so much pleasure, he couldn't get his body to move.

☐●☐●☐●☐

GRACE FELT HERSELF SLIPPING, FALLING deeper into the moment with these two men. This was incredible and unbelievable all at the same time. She was being pressed into the mattress beneath Lane's big body while Grant was folded over Lane, forcing Lane deeper inside of her.

"Please move," she moaned, wanting to feel the glorious friction that she'd felt when Lane first entered her. "I need to feel you."

Lane stared back at her. He seemed dazed, although he still donned that Oscar worthy smile.

But he didn't move.

She peered over Lane's shoulder, her eyes meeting Grant's. He smiled back at her, although it seemed a little strained. She realized he was hanging on the same way she was – by his fingernails.

"Please," she whispered to him and then suddenly there was movement.

Glorious, amazing, wonderful friction ignited her nerve endings, lighting her up from the inside out as she held onto Lane. Grant's hands were circling her ankles and the idea that they were both touching her, both making love to her at the exact same time sent her plummeting over the edge without warning. She cried out as her body spasmed out of control, eliciting a tortured growl from Lane.

"Oh, damn. Gracie, baby…" Lane's lips found hers, and Grace held on for dear life as both men began to move. She didn't know how they did it, not sure how they found a rhythm that would work for all of them, but they did.

"I want you to come again," Grant told her, his eyes locked with hers when Lane pulled back, the muscles in Lane's arms straining to hold himself above her.

"Yes," she agreed. She wanted that, too.

An explosion of movement had her gripping the comforter, trying to hold herself in place as Lane rocked into her while Grant slammed into him from behind. It was... perfect.

And then, yes, once again she was spiraling. There wasn't anything sweet about her orgasm. It took root and exploded, magnificent, resplendent sensation tore through her, shot out through her fingertips and her toes as she came in a rush.

Above her, Lane stilled, his face taut, his eyes pinning her in place before they closed.

"Oh, fuck yes, Gracie. Grant," he growled, and Grace felt him pulse inside of her.

"Yes, that's it. Come for me," Grant chanted, and then he was coming violently; his beautiful body hovering above them, his chest slick from sweat, his dark hair mussed and his eyes boring into her. "God, yes."

At that moment, Grace was almost positive that Grant mouthed the words I love you. She wasn't absolutely positive, but it was enough to send another tremor through her.

CHAPTER EIGHT

THE FOLLOWING MORNING, AFTER HE had managed to pry himself out of bed, Grant had dressed quickly and quietly and headed for the main house. Breakfast. That's what he was in search of. Enough to take back to Gracie's for the three of them.

The three of them.

A warmth spread through Grant's chest as he opened the screen door and slipped into the cool, open breakfast room that held a variety of items for the guests and employees.

He'd spent the night entwined with Lane and Gracie after the three of them had shared a quick shower in Gracie's miniscule bathroom, a peace unlike anything he'd ever known engulfing him every moment that he was with them both. When they'd turned to one another in the dim room somewhere close to dawn, he'd been overwhelmed with so much emotion, he was surprised he'd been able to do anything.

But he had. This time he'd been the one to slide into Gracie ever so slowly while she wrapped herself around him. Lane had curled up against them, forgoing intercourse in exchange for watching them. Grant had clutched Lane's hand, holding on while he made love to Gracie slowly. It had been powerful.

And although Grant had mouthed the words he wanted to shout to the universe, he hadn't heard them in return. But as much as he wanted to hear them, he knew that Gracie and Lane both felt something. Something more than just pleasure for the sake of pleasure.

"What's up, cowboy?"

Grant glanced over to see Mercy standing beside him as he piled pastries onto a paper plate.

"Hungry this morning, huh?"

He didn't answer her. He couldn't.

"It's cool, you know. It's been a long time coming."

Grant turned to face her, trying to pretend he had no idea what she was talking about. A quick survey of the room told him they were far enough away that no one had overheard her. Not that anyone would know what she was talking about anyway.

"Just don't hurt her," Mercy paused, reached for a muffin before meeting his gaze once again, "Or him."

Grant swallowed hard. How the hell... Was it that fucking obvious?

He didn't get a chance to ask Mercy that question because she turned and sauntered away, saying good morning to the handful of guests who'd trickled in before the sun was fully up in the sky.

Scared that someone else was going to question him and ultimately know that he'd spent the night with Lane and Gracie, Grant took the plate and made a beeline for the back door.

□●□●□●□

GRACE WOKE UP WITH A warm body snuggled up against her back. She didn't move immediately, instead opened her eyes and looked at the door that led to the living room.

She knew where she was. And she knew who was there. Through the night, she'd become familiar enough with both Lane and Grant that she could tell the difference in their touch. It was strange, but oddly comforting at the same time.

Oh, yes, she knew without a doubt that she was hopelessly in love with both men. Over the moon. But that hadn't stopped the fear from taking control of her mind. What were people going to think? This was her family's ranch. Lane and Grant worked for her father. And her father had made a point over the years to warn the cowboys away from his daughters repeatedly.

Not that the cowboys listened. Grace happened to know for a fact that each of her sisters had been intimately involved with at least one man who worked on the ranch at some point. And now, she knew that there were a couple of cowboys sniffing around her sisters again.

As she lay there, her hands resting on Lane's arm that was wrapped around her, she looked up to see Grant now standing in the doorway. She hadn't even realized he was gone, but yes, there he was in all of his handsome glory. He looked... sad.

"What's the matter?" she whispered, hoping not to wake Lane.

Too late.

He stirred behind her, his arm pulling her closer to him while he lifted his head from the pillow they were sharing. "You okay?" he asked Grant.

Grant nodded as he moved into the room, quickly shunning his clothes as he moved toward them.

Once he was naked, he crawled into the bed facing Grace, sandwiching her between them.

"I've never been better," he told them.

Why didn't she believe him?

Afraid of ruining the moment, Grace didn't ask the inevitable question. She just stared back at him. For now, this was going to be all right. The rest of the world was safely locked outside, and she could enjoy the warmth of these two men for the today and maybe tomorrow.

And Monday, she'd worry about that then.

Because until they had to face the harsh realities of the real world, nothing else mattered.

□●□●□●□

LANE FELT THE TENSION IN the air around him. He could see it in the way Grant moved, in the way he looked at them. Fear was already setting in.

He fully understood that fear. Fear of what tomorrow would bring. Fear that they'd lose this moment and never recapture it.

Last night had been perfect. In fact, it had been so incredible that when they found each other in the early morning hours, he'd been so overcome with emotion that he'd had to sit back and claim to only want to watch. These two moved him in ways he never expected.

Well, actually he had expected it. From the moment he met them. Lane wasn't one to fall in love easily, but he'd been in love – at least a little bit – with both of them for so long that this just felt normal. But it wasn't normal. At least not by everyone's standards and he knew that's what Grant was worried about. He could see it in the man's stormy blue eyes.

Grant was thinking too much.

Wanting to erase the shadows he saw in Grant's eyes, Lane willed him to look at him. And almost as though he could feel his request, Grant looked away from Gracie and up at him.

"I love you," Lane said, putting it all out there. "I love you both."

"I –" they both said simultaneously.

"No, wait," Lane interrupted. "I'm not asking you to say anything back. I just needed you both to know. It's true. It's always been true." Lane hated that his emotions were getting the best of him, but he forced himself to continue. "I don't want this to end. Ever. But, I'm not naïve enough to think it won't be hard. I just want you both to know that it can be done. If we want it enough, it can be done."

Neither of them spoke, but Gracie shifted so that she was looking up at them. There were tears in her eyes and Lane leaned down and pressed his lips to hers.

"I want it enough," she told him, a mere whisper against his lips.

Lane lifted his head and met Grant's eyes. He didn't speak, but he nodded his head.

And right then and there, Lane knew that they could make this work. They would make it work.

There were a few obstacles that they would need to overcome first. It was just going to take some time.

And he was all right with that because he had all the time in the world. And loving both of them would only make that time pass much more easily.

CHAPTER NINE

MERCY LAMBERT SAT AT THE table in the crowded dining room, trying to ignore all that was going on around her. She just wanted to finish her breakfast and sneak out before anyone paid her too much attention.

"Hey, Merce."

The deep voice sounded from behind her and Mercy tensed, an automatic response to the one man she tried to avoid on the best of days.

"Mind if I join you?"

Mercy looked up into Cody Mercer's startlingly brilliant green eyes. Doing her best not to shake her head no, she darted her eyes toward the chair on the opposite side of the table.

The man didn't take the hint.

No, Cody wasn't the type of guy to let her put too much distance between them, no matter how hard she tried. And yes, Mercy tried pretty damn hard.

Proof in point, Mercy turned her attention to the bland eggs and rubbery bacon that sat on her plate. Their cook needed a stern talking to because he was falling down on the job, which wasn't doing a damn thing for her appetite. And Lord knew, she needed to eat because she was about to spend the next six or so hours out in the heat, probably without a minute to spare for lunch.

Okay, so yes, she was avoiding this man. So much so that she was studying the consistency of the eggs, separating them with her fork, making sure to slide the fork across the glass plate, emitting an ear splitting sound.

Anything to keep from looking up into that incredibly handsome face.

"Still not talkin' to me, huh?" Cody asked, sounding as confident as he usually did.

"Tryin' not to," she answered, still not looking up at him. "You make it damn hard to succeed."

"That's the plan." The rich, deep laugh that echoed through the oversized dining area made Mercy's insides tingle.

Damn him.

She did not want to be attracted to this guy. She did not want to sit there and have a normal conversation with him. And by God, she did not want to remember the one night they spent together not that long ago, both of them sweaty and slick as she rode him like a fucking cowgirl right there in the garage that housed the heavy equipment that he worked on.

"You'll come around, I'm sure," Cody said softly, setting his coffee mug on the table, his hand grazing hers as he pulled away.

Mercy jerked her head up, pinning him with a glare that she hoped was evil enough to send him toppling over in his chair.

Son of a bitch.

Cody smiled. And damn him all to hell, she loved that sexy little smirk that curled the left side of his mouth, exposing that damned dimple that she found so damned attractive.

Damn.

Okay, and now her vocabulary had been reduced to that of one of the redneck cowboys she came in contact with generally when she was down at Whiskeys, the only bar within a ten mile radius. The one she was already making plans to visit in the very, very near future. Hell, at this rate, who needed to wait until five o'clock?

"Come on, babe, when are you going to get over the fact that I rocked your world and you liked it?"

When Cody went to touch her hand again, Mercy picked up her fork and stabbed the table, mere centimeters from where he'd just been. His eyes opened wide and it was her turn to smirk. "In your dreams, cowboy," she said, keeping her voice as low as she could.

But then that damn smirk on his face was back and Mercy felt an answering tug deep in her womb.

Yep, she was pretty damned sure that she'd found something she never, not in her wildest dreams, expected to find on this ranch...

Her Kryptonite.

Dear reader,

I hope you enjoyed the introduction to the sweet, sultry Lambert sisters and the sexy cowboys they love. Don't worry; there'll be plenty more of Lane, Grant and Gracie in book 1 of the Dead Heat Ranch series, ***Betting on Grace,*** scheduled for release on July 29, 2014.

Keep reading for an excerpt! Enjoy!

Book One

August, one month later

Monday morning

"Where're you headed?" Lane Miller hollered from the south end of Dead Heat Ranch's main barn.

Lane had walked into the enormous steel building just in time to see, through a hazy dust-mote stream lit by the rays from the early-morning sun, Grant Kingsley high-tailing it across the marred concrete floor. Grant was moving like his ass was on fire, which was, quite frankly, a sight to see.

With the sound of Lane's heavy footsteps resounding off the metal walls, a few goats bleating their morning greeting, and the scent of manure and hay flooding his nostrils, Lane picked up his pace, attempting to keep up with Grant before he hit the wide-open double doors on the opposite end.

Lane was halfway across the barn when he noticed that, in his haste to ensnare the hunky cowboy trying to evade him, he had captured the attention of Budweiser, one of the three Labrador retrievers that lived on the ranch. The charming black dog ran toward him, tongue lolling, tail wagging, but Lane didn't pause to pet him as he normally would, fearful that Grant would disappear if he veered off course.

"Asking a question here!" Lane yelled, trying to get Grant to stop. "Where're you off to?" he repeated.

"Runnin' into town."

For a fraction of a second, Lane wondered if Grant meant *literally* because of the fast pace he was maintaining. Doubtful, but the mental image was quite amusing. And picturing Grant huffing it into town sure beat thinking about the way Grant had answered. Grant had drawled the response as though he didn't have a care in the world; however, he didn't bother to spare Lane a glance, which was Lane's first hint that something was up.

Hell, for as much attention as Grant was giving him, Lane could've been anyone, certainly not someone who was actually supposed to be important to Grant.

Drop it, Miller. Not gonna get you anywhere today. Chin up.

Doing his best to heed his own advice, Lane set off in a half jog, half run, in order to catch Grant before he got too far away. Budweiser, of course, thought it was a game and trotted alongside him, barking happily.

"Hey," Lane called to Grant again, trying to get him to slow his roll. It didn't seem to be working, so he glanced down at the animal scurrying along beside him. "Mornin', Budweiser," he muttered to the dog, earning another enthusiastic woof from the animal.

Well, at least someone was paying attention to Lane.

"What?" Grant exclaimed a little unexpectedly, and Lane hauled his gaze back up, where he saw that, yes, Grant had actually stopped walking.

Finally.

When Grant spun around to face him, Lane came to a jerky stop, surprised by the irritated expression on Grant's too-handsome face.

"You okay?" Lane asked, concerned, standing less than a foot away from the man who, in recent weeks, had sent Lane's entire world on its ear.

In a good way.

"Yeah. Fine. What do you need?"

Okay, so someone was lying, and since Lane wasn't the one spouting off that he was fine when he clearly wasn't, the award went to Grant.

"What's your problem?" Lane mouthed off, getting a little defensive.

It wasn't that he was surprised that Grant was in a foul mood; after all, this was Grant. He wasn't *always* chipper, but that hadn't been the case so much lately. In fact, Grant had been the picture of sunshine for the last few months, and Lane wanted to think that he played at least a small part in that. Rightfully so, Lane hadn't expected to be met with such animosity that early in the morning.

"I've got things to do, Lane, what the hell do you want?"

Lane glanced just past Grant's head, making sure they were alone, not wanting to risk someone stumbling upon them when he...

"Oomph."

Lane pushed Grant's lean body up against the inside wall of the barn, successfully slipping into the shadows before he crushed his mouth down on Grant's in a kiss that threatened to spark the dry hay stored there into an inferno. Again, Budweiser thought it was time to play, pawing at Lane's ass as Lane took control of the kiss, cupping Grant's stubble-covered jaw as he leaned into him.

Despite the attitude, Grant pretty much turned to putty in his arms, and Lane didn't let up, sliding his tongue into the hot cavern of Grant's mouth. He trailed his hands down Grant's neck, over the hard planes of Grant's chest, across his rippled abs, then lower until he was gripping Grant's narrow hips. Lane held him in place, rocking his erection against Grant's through the confining denim of their jeans, trying to get as close as physically possible because... Well, just fucking because.

Grant Kingsley was like rocket fuel, combustible and capable of intense heat. Even now, when it was clear Grant was inspired by something more than lust, if his sour mood was anything to go by, the man pretty much went up in flames right there in Lane's arms. Even with Grant's grumpy attitude, Lane found that he craved the man like a drug.

Grant's fingers knotted in the front of Lane's T-shirt as the other man pulled him closer, sending Lane's head whirling. Hot damn, it had been too long since they'd done this. *This* being sharing a kiss that made bright, colorful lights dance behind Lane's closed eyelids.

Another few heated moments passed while Lane tried to get his fix, plunging his tongue into Grant's mouth, tasting the coffee his lover must've had a short while ago, and desperately wishing they had just a little more privacy than the shadowed interior of the main barn.

No such luck, which was why Lane reluctantly drew back.

"Good mornin'," Lane said to Grant with a grin, still holding Grant's hip with one hand while absently patting Budweiser's big head as the insistent animal pushed his snout up against Lane's leg, begging for attention.

Grant rolled his eyes, but Lane was pretty sure that was a smile that curled the very corners of Grant's delicious mouth.

"What're you goin' into town for?" Lane asked curiously, forcing himself to take another step back, releasing Grant from his clutches despite his desire to slam his mouth on Grant's one more time for good measure.

"My dad called," Grant disclosed, a flicker of heat mixed with what Lane could only assume was aggravation — based on Grant's tone — glimmering in his ocean-blue eyes.

"Your dad's not *in* town, Grant," Lane offered helpfully, not telling Grant anything he didn't already know.

Lane wasn't up to speed on everything about Grant's parents, but he was aware that they lived nearly an hour *outside* of town, which meant that Grant's "in town" reference was supposed to deter Lane.

"No shit, Sherlock," Grant bit back.

"So what does he want?" Lane asked, pretending not to be bothered by Grant's snippy fucking attitude.

As with Grant's parents' whereabouts, Lane didn't know much about Grant's rapport with his folks, either, but from what Lane had gathered over the years, their relationship was strained at best.

"I need to stop by and talk to him."

Now Lane's Spidey senses were beginning to go off, and Grant wasn't helping with his elusive retort. "Need" was a pretty strong word, especially when Grant used it.

Grant wasn't much for running off to deal with personal business, nor was he usually quick to share the details of his life, but Lane figured it was safe to assume they had crossed a particular line in recent months. The one they no longer saw in their peripheral vision because they'd taken a few steps forward and zero steps back. And Lane wanted to believe that once they passed that line and it disappeared from view, it was only fair that they were expected to open up a little more than normal.

Someone probably needed to remind Grant of that because apparently he was regressing.

"What's up, man? Talk to me."

Grant met his gaze, and this time Lane saw defiance there.

Fucking hell.

Scratch that. Grant wasn't *regressing*; he was running backward at lightning speed.

"Don't make me kiss it outta you," Lane threatened, doing his best to keep the happy-go-lucky tone he was known for.

"As much as I'd like that," Grant said hesitantly, his eyes darting across their immediate surroundings, passing over Budweiser, who was still watching them intently, before meeting Lane's once more, "I really do need to go."

"Fine." It was clear that Grant wasn't going to delve into the specifics about what was bothering him. At least not out there in the dusty barn.

Bearing in mind how much physical distance they had inserted between the three of them — him, Grant, *and* Gracie — in recent weeks, due to circumstances out of their control, Lane knew not to push his luck.

No, he would corner Grant later and kiss it out of him — just as he'd threatened — if he had to.

But for now, he opted to change the subject. "How 'bout dinner?"

Grant's eyes softened somewhat, but that was as far as Lane was going to let him go because he knew what was coming. Regressing had quickly turned to retreating, and now Grant was backsliding at a rapid pace. Lane had feared it was coming for the last couple of weeks.

Clamping his hand over Grant's mouth before the man could give him some sorry excuse, Lane said, "Don't do this. Don't come up with some bullshit reason to push me away. You hear me? We've come too damn far for this." Lane stared back at Grant for a long moment. "I'm going to work, and you're gonna be on your way. Whatever you think you want right now, you'd better give it some more thought. I'm not gonna drop this, so don't even ask me to."

Grant's eyes were wide by the time Lane released his mouth. And just like he said he would, Lane turned on his heel and walked away.

Right after he pressed his lips to Grant's for a quick, potent kiss.

Grace Lambert was coming out of the six-thousand-square-foot main house, where pretty much all business-related activities associated with Dead Heat Ranch occurred, including the Monday morning meetings she had with her father and sisters, at about the same time Lane was going in. Where her head was at, she had no idea, but before she knew it, she was on a collision course with the delectable cowboy. The same cowboy who made her heart burst into a full gallop every time she saw him. The same one who, just a few months ago, she had tried to steer clear of.

Yeah, that ship had obviously sailed.

"Well, hello, gorgeous," Lane said huskily when she found herself flush against him, one hand clutching his huge bicep, the other crushed between them — the only thing saving her iPhone from a header on the wooden deck that wrapped around the house.

Their close proximity would likely appear an accidental collision to an onlooker, but based on the way Lane slid his hands along her hips, his chest pressed firmly against her breasts, what had started out innocent took a quick and abrupt turn to the lascivious.

Mmm… Lascivious. Some seriously delicious moments that they had shared over the last few months came to mind.

Grace didn't mind the close contact, although she prayed no one was paying any attention. Because if they were…

Stumbling back a step or two just in case someone did have them in their cross hairs, Grace shifted her attention from the phone in her hand to the devastatingly handsome cowboy in front of her. "Sorry," she muttered shyly, her face warming several degrees.

"Babe, feel free to knock me off my feet anytime you want. This certainly isn't the first time."

Unable to help herself, she smiled up at him. Way up.

Grace knew she wasn't even average when it came to her height of five feet four inches, although she was taller than her four sisters, but compared to Lane's six-foot-three-inch frame, she felt impossibly small.

"Someone's in a good mood this mornin'," she offered.

"Wish I could say the same."

"What's with you people today? You'd think it was Monday or somethin'."

"It *is* Monday, Lane," Grace informed Lane with a full-fledged smile.

"Oh. Well, hell. That explains it then. Where'd the weekend go?"

"No idea. I think I worked through it."

"Yep, I know the feelin'."

It had been an incredibly busy few weeks for all of them. With the official end of summer nearing as August came to a close, things seemed to be moving at warp speed. The days were tirelessly long and seemingly endless, with all of the guests who were cramming in a last-minute summer vacation before school was back in session.

Thanks to the steady influx of tourists visiting, they'd spent the last two months performing some much-needed updates on the ranch. They had worked continuously to get everything done in a short amount of time, including getting two of the extra cabins in tip-top shape so they could be occupied, providing the on-site store with a much-needed facelift, installing some new commercial appliances in the kitchen, and replacing a handful of the wobbly old tables scattered throughout the dining area. Not to mention all of the new things going on with the actual animals that were supposed to be the primary focus of their day-to-day chores.

They had recently purchased six new horses for the ranch, specifically to use for the tourist trail rides, and they'd all been pitching in with getting them acquainted with the ranch. Dixie, their beloved yellow Labrador, had inadvertently gotten herself knocked up by Budweiser a couple of months back, and they were all required to be on puppy duty as well.

It didn't help that Hope, Grace's older sister, was off on some crazy rampage about increasing the ranch's income potential. The spur in her sister's butt had caused a hiring trend during peak season, along with a shitload of new activities put in place for the guests.

"Gotta spend money to make money," Hope had spouted when they'd questioned her recent spending spree.

As far as Grace was concerned, they were doing just fine, thank you very much. Not that she was responsible for the books or anything. But Faith, the youngest of the five of them, was. And according to Faith, they were in the black, which was all Grace really cared to hear.

Possibly not for long if Hope had her way.

"Have you talked to Grant today?" Lane asked abruptly, pulling Grace from her thoughts.

"No." Shoving her phone in her back pocket, Grace gave Lane her full attention. Just the mention of Grant had piqued her curiosity.

It'd been at least three days since she'd spent any time with him, and even then, they hadn't been able to get much more than a stolen kiss or two on the go. It had been late every night when Grace finally managed to drag her ass home, desperate for a hot shower and a good eight hours of shut-eye. She'd managed the shower but not much on the sleep, because morning had come far too quickly every damned time.

Unfortunately, spending time with Lane and Grant in the last few weeks had been sporadic at best. Not because she didn't want to. Quite the contrary, actually.

Regrettably, life had kicked back in, insinuating itself right smack in the middle of the new relationship that she'd formed with the two men not long ago. Since they were all tiptoeing around in order to ensure her father didn't catch wind of what was going on with them, they'd had to perform a few evasive maneuvers recently just to throw him off their scent. Jerry Lambert was not an easy man to avoid, either.

Damn Mercy.

One of Grace's sisters had caught on to what was going on between the three of them probably before they'd even known it themselves, and now Grace feared Mercy was going to use it against her.

Not that she would let Mercy know that she actually cared who found out. She really didn't.

Well, no one except for her father. Jerry was a bear of a man, and he had growled his demands on more than one occasion for the cowboys at Dead Heat Ranch to keep their hands off his daughters. Any man caught touching one of them would risk his wrath.

Yeah, well...

If her father knew that there were *two* cowboys touching her specifically, he'd probably have a coronary.

"He mentioned that he had to go see his dad," Lane stated.

"Really? His dad?" she asked, shocked.

"Yeah. He wouldn't go into detail, but something was off."

"They don't get along," Grace said, figuring Lane already knew as much.

"I got that part. I know he doesn't go see them often, but this seemed like a demand, not a request."

Grace didn't know what to make of that. She didn't know much about Grant's parents, just that Grant's relationship with them was tense. Come to think of it, Grace didn't know much about Lane's parents, either.

Wow. For a woman who was sexually intimate with two men at one time, she'd just realized how little she actually knew about them. Then again, that was mostly her fault because she'd spent the last couple of years avoiding them at all costs.

What the hell did that say about her?

Oh, who really cared?

"Did he say when he was coming back?"

"Nope. And when I suggested dinner, he blew me off."

Grace could tell that Lane was holding something back, but she didn't get a chance to question him about it because — speak of the devil — her sister Mercy came walking up.

"Time to get to work, kiddos. No smoochin' on company time."

"Shut up," Grace bit out, sounding like a petulant, irritable child. Feeling like one, too.

Mercy brought out the best in her, clearly.

Grace was met with a shit-eating grin from her sister.

"Sorry, no can do. I'm comin' to let you know that we've got a family meetin' goin' on in just a few minutes."

"What? Another one?" Grace hadn't heard about another meeting. Hell, she'd just wasted the better part of an hour listening to Faith give them a stern talking-to about spending money.

"Yep, Hope's on a tangent. She wants to hire three more people. Time to talk it out."

"Where?"

"At the rec hall," Mercy said as she turned to face Lane. "And as much as we'd love to see your bright, shinin' face there, you're not invited. Not unless you've proposed to my sister and now I get to call you Bubba."

Lane smiled, which put Grace on high alert.

"Not yet, ma'am," Lane drawled. "But trust me, when it comes to that, I'll be sure to let you know."

Grace's head twisted around on her body hard enough to give herself whiplash. "Lane!" she yelled. "No more fuel for the fire, please!"

Just as he always did, Lane brushed off her warning. The guy didn't seem to have a care in the world. She had to wonder just what he'd say if her father were to confront him on some statement like that.

The sound of the screen door slamming behind Grace told her that Mercy had moved on.

Thank God.

"I've gotta run. We've got a group comin' in around noon, and I need to help out. How 'bout dinner?" Lane spoke to her directly, but he might as well have been talking to the whole damn ranch for as quiet as he was.

"We'll see," Grace said, tempted to search their surroundings, wanting to ensure some nosy-ass wrangler wasn't passing by.

"In my book, 'we'll see' is the equivalent of yes. I'll bring dinner to your place. How's that sound?"

Grace was just about to lay into him when he pulled her up against him, his mouth finding hers. "Your sister's gone, and there ain't another soul anywhere close."

Grace couldn't help it; she turned to liquid in his arms. As much as she wanted to punch him for freaking her out like that, she damn sure enjoyed when he put his mouth on hers. Or anywhere, for that matter.

"Gotta run, gorgeous," Lane said as he backed away slowly, his mocha-brown eyes peering into hers. Grace wanted to grab his arm and pull him into a dark corner somewhere for a few minutes of catching up, but she didn't.

She was restraining herself and all.

Something she found was getting more and more difficult as each day passed, especially the days when she didn't get to spend *any* time with Lane or Grant, or, which she preferred most, both of them at the same time.

"Dinner," Lane called out when he was several yards away. "Your place. I'll bring the food."

Grace nodded, praying like hell that no one was listening because...

Yeah, they were really going to have to do something about this sneaking around thing.

And soon.

The Devil's Playground Series
Without Regret
Without Restraint

The Office Intrigue Duet
Office Intrigue
Intrigued Out of the Office
Their Rebellious Submissive

The Pier 70 Series
Reckless
Fearless
Speechless
Harmless

The Sniper 1 Security Series
Wait for Morning
Never Say Never

The Southern Boy Mafia Series
Beautifully Brutal
Beautifully Loyal

Standalone Novels
A Million Tiny Pieces
Inked on Paper

Writing as Timberlyn Scott
Unhinged
Unraveling
Chaos

Naughty Holiday Editions
2015
2016

Made in the USA
Monee, IL
10 June 2020